MW00768689

Their Kind

To: Terri
Happy Mother's
Day too you.
thank you for being
the friend to my
daughter that she
deserves in her life
have blue. I love you
Retha Richardson

Retha M. Richardson

Copyright © 2016 Retha M. Richardson
All rights reserved.

ISBN: 1530100658
ISBN 13: 9781530100651
Library of Congress Control Number: 2016902835
CreateSpace Independent Publishing Platform
North Charleston, South Carolina

INTRODUCTION

THE THEIRKINDS ARE FICTTIONAL CREATURES THAT POSSESS DIFFERENT ABILITIES. IT'S THE YEAR 3052. THEY LIVE ON AN ISLAND CALLED WILLOWEIST PLACE OUT IN THE MIDDLE OF THE OCEAN. THIS IS WHERE SOCIAL SEGREGATION IS LAW AND ARE STRICTLY ENFORCED. THESE LAWS WERE PUT IN PLACE, BY THE ONE EYES, TO SERVE THE FEW AND CONTROL THE MANY. THE ONE EYES CAME TO THE ISLAND AS FUGITIVES, OUTCASTS, BANDED FROM THEIR OWN LAND. THEY SHOWED UP ON WILLOWEIST ONE DAY, HIDING THEIR AGENDAS, WHICH WAS TO TAKE OVER. WITH POLITENESS, KIND WORDS, AND SMILES. THEY EVENTUALLY TOOK OVER THE ISLAND BY FORCE, ERASED THE HISTORY OF WILLOWEIST, AND MADE UP A COMPLETELY DIFFERENT HISTORY. THESE LIES, WERE WRITTEN IN BOOKS, AND TAUGHT AS TRUTH. THEY CONSIDER THEMSELVES THE LEADERS OF THE ISLAND. AND THEY CONTROL ALL OF THE BUSINESS ASPECTS OF THE ISLAND. THEY LIVE VERY AFLUENT LIFES WHICH HAS AFFORDED THEM MUCH, WHILE THE VASE MAJORITY OF THE INHABITIANTS, LIVE VERY BASIC LIVES. UNKNOWING TO ALL OF THE WILLOWEISTIANS, FAMILIAR WINDS CAN CHANGE.

THE THEIR-KINDS

THE FIRST GROUP AS MENTIONED EARLIER ARE THE ONE EYES. THEY CONSIDER THEMSELVES THE ELITIST. THEY HAVE ONE VISION AND NO SIGHT. THEY WERE THE LAST GROUP TO OCCUPY THE ISLAND. THEIR ONE EYE REPRESENTS ONE FOCUS, ONE MOTIVE, AND ONE MISSION THAT IS TO CONQUER AND RULE THROUGHT GREED AND SEVER PARANOIA. THE NEXT

*GROUP IS CALLED THE TWO EYES. ONE EYE IS FOR SIGHT AND THE OTHER IS A VISION FOR COMPASSION FOR OTHERS. THEY LIVE OFF LESS AND ARE TYPICAL OF WHAT THE MIDDLE CLASS WOULD BE IN MOST SOCIETIES. THEN LAST AND CERTAINLY LEAST ARE THE THREE EYED THEIRKINDS. THEY HAVE ONE EYE FOR SIGHT, ONE FOR COMPASSION FOR OTHERS, AND ONE FOR SPIRITUAL INSIGHT. THEY ARE THE MOST OUTCASTED AMONG THE ISLANDERS. AND ARE CONSIDERED OUTCASTS, INSANE, WITCH CRAFTERS. THEY WORK THE HARDEST AND MAKE THE LEAST ON THE ISLAND. BUT THEY ARE SURVIVORS. SO COME ALONG FOR A PERSONAL INTRODUCTION ONTO THE WORLD OF THE THEIRKINDS. **PERFECT** IS A ONE EYED FEMALE. SHE'S A SWEET YOUNG LADY THAT'S ATTENDING COLLEGE. NEXT IS **KILGOR**, HE'S PERFECTS FATHER AND AN AFLUENT ONE EYE AND DEDICATED MEMBER OF WILLOWEIST COUNCIL. **PATSY** IS PERFECTS MOM ONE EYED WOMAN. A VERY SWEET WOMAN BUT CLOSES HER EYE TO ANY AND ALL THINGS SHE DOES NOT WANT TO DEAL WITH. SHE LIVES IN HER PERFECT WORLD UNDISTURBED. THEN NEXT THERE'S **NERVIUS** HIS IS A ONE EYED THEIRKIND GUY, HE ATTENDS COLLEGE WITH PERFECT. NEXT IS **SIN** SHE IS A ONE EYED THEIRKIND WOMAN ATTENDING SCHOOL AS WELL. SHE'S VERY SEDUCTIVE IN APPEARANCE AND LIVES UP TO HER NAME. NEXT IS **CIUEY** SHE IS A ONE EYED FELMALE THEIRKIND. SHE ALSO ATTENDS THE UNIVERSITY. SHE'S PERFECT'S BEST FRIEND. SHE LIVES A CARBON COPY IMAGE OF PERFECT'S LIFE. NEXT IS **MARLEY** A MIDDLE AGE TWO EYED THEIRKIND WIDOW, A CAREGIVER. AND THE CORNERSTORNE OF HER COMMUNITY.*

THE BABIES

MERCY IS A TWO EYED LITTLE BOY. HE IS PERFECT AND NERVIUS'S SON. *GRACE* IS A THREE EYED LITTLE GIRL. *FAVOR* IS A LITTLE FOUR EYED MALE. THEY ALL ARE SO PRECIOUS AND SO SPECIAL!

Dedication

Throughout this wonderful yet trying journey I have very special people that I would like to dedicate this book to. First and for most I dedicate this book too my life's source. THE ALMIGHTY GOD JEHOVA, MY LORD AND SAVOIR JESUS CHIRST that died for my sins, and the sins of the world. For without them I would be noth-ing. This book was written so that before the world He will receive the glory. Now earth bound I dedicate this book also to my sweetheart and beloved husband the late Kevin C. Richardson. He kept me inspired and motivated. I love you my darling. I dedicate this book to my parents the late Willie D. Beavers Sr. and the late Lugenner M. Beavers for without them I would not exist. Thank you mom and dad for all the love and valuable life lessons. My mentors and supporters were my sister in-law Stephanie Conyers a very talented accomplished writer in her own right, with loving encouragement, and great support she helped to guide me through this process. Thank you so much. My friend and mentor Mrs. Melony Samuels that has also been a great support, recognized my talent before I did, when it was still in the developmental stages, she guided me. She is a master in stage plays, casting, writing, and production. Next my beloved family my daughter, Mrs. Genner Hunter and her husband Montae

Hunter, my son John Fendall II and his fiancée' Tiffany, my niece Sherell Rosson that's like a daughter to me. My beautiful grandchildren Avian, Aniya Hunt, my great nieces Nadia and Naomi. The support of my siblings. My brother Alantino Beavers for being my cartoonist. Thank you all for your love and support.

.

"Faith will never take you where God's Mercy, Grace, and Favor will not keep you".

-By Retha Richardson

Contents

1

Graduation Trip

*I*t's in the spring of the year, on the sleepy island of Willowiest. The young one eyed Theirkinds at Prestige University College, are getting ready to graduate. Excitement is in the air. One Eyed Theirkinds parents are bustling along, making their arrival preparations, for this upcoming afternoon's event. The young Theirkinds have completed their accomplishments of learning. Now they will be stepping across into a world where, they will be in control of their lives, and totally independent of the parents. Around the campus nature is blooming in all its glory has a crisp newness to life has filled the air. Perfect is among the young promising graduates. She a good girl, ambitious, smart, and curious about life. She especially loves mystery and adventure. Perfect's parents are well connected, and well established. Her father Kilgore is one of the councilmen for Willowiest. Her main college buddies are Cluey, Nervius, and Sin.

Perfect has known Cluey since their childhood. She met Nervius and Sin when she began college. Cluey's family owns all of the grocery chains, on the island. Cluey is a sweet, slang, harmless, soul with a little wild side to her. Sin is their mutual friend she's very mysterious, cold, with, a cunning mentality. Nervius is the first male friend Perfect met at school. Nervius is a guy that just wants to live well and have fun in the moment. He was in a very bad car accident a few years ago, His best friend was killed. He made a full recovery from his injuries, but it left him with a large unsightly scar on one side of his face. He made up his mind after that, to enroll himself in school, so he started attending the University. Those years passed quickly for them, now the four are anxiously awaiting this proud day, when they will walk across the stage, and receive their degrees. The campus is humming with all the last minute details. A sea of white chairs are carefully aligned, across the west lawn of the school's campus. 500 strong will finally make their way across the stage to get their well-earned degrees. Guests are still arriving, with invitations in hand, programs are stacked, and ready to be passed out. Special parking permits were issued to monitor the number of guest attending. With most elite Theirkinds arriving in style security will need to be vigilant at all times. Perfect, Cluey, Sin, and Nervius are planning, as many other graduates, to take a well-deserved graduation trip, to celebrated their milestone. Graduation is about an hour away and everyone is getting dressed, grooming themselves, or on their way to the commencement area. The ceremony was long, getting through all the guest speakers, awards presentations, and acknowledgements. But it was a success, everything went off without a hitch. Partying perused shortly after the commencement, and it lasted throughout the night. At first light, the four friends were on a cruise ship the next morning to a neighboring island called Jessup. Jessup is an island used as a vacation spot for the neighboring Willowiestians. Jessup by boat is about three hours. They arrived safely, Perfect, Cluey, and Sin clear's customs in a synch. Because One Eyed Theirkinds only needed to do a pupil scan and they were into the country no *with problem. Nervius had a small problem his pupil scan it would not work. So they processed him the old fashion way by stamping his passport and they were in and on their way. The four collected their bags, proceeded to the shuttle, and then onto their resort. They checked into their rooms, changed into their swim suites, and were back down stairs in a matter of minutes, to enjoy the activities at their luxury resort. The view from any angle was simply magnificent. There were live entertainment, volley ball games, beach cook outs, parasailing, water skiing, and everything one could imagine to enjoy. They got their drinks at the bar and retreated to the beach area. They found their spots on the beach. They were all aligned side by side, under one large grass umbrella, on their beach chairs. Perfect asked; hey guys maybe later we can play volley ball or perhaps we could go water skiing? They all nodded okay. Just then someone on a parasail drifts right over their heads. All four heads were up off of the beach chairs watching the parasailer until he was out of sight. Nervius pipes up; Wow that looks so cool. I would like to do that. Perfect says sure you can. Sin looks over to her left and there were two young Theirkinds, necking making out, under their umbrella. She chuckles and nudges Perfect, Perfect nudges Cluey, and they all burst out laughing. Sin turns on her side toward Cluey and Perfect and whispers; Hey have either of you ever made out with a guy? Cluey and Perfect looked bashful and surprised at the same time. They both says no at the same time, then they all burst out laughing again. Cluey pipes up; well Sin have you ever made out with a guy? Sin smiles and says; well of course I have. I look at it like this. Why should I take a chance on saving myself for a husband just to find out he might really suck. Sin then reaches in her beach bag and pulled out a small plastic bag and a pack of small green paper leaves. She sits up on her beach chair starts to make herself an old fashion cigarette, she lights it and begins smoking it. Perfect asked her; what is that? Sin responses; it's Sash. Sin rolls her eye. Don't tell me you all have never smoked Sash? Perfect and Cluey both shakes their heads no. Sin offers; here it's just an herb, it's all natural, it'll help you to relax.*

They still refuse. She offers some to Nervius. He sits up and takes it from her and takes a pull. Nervius says coughing; hey ladies it's good, it want hurt you, just get you high, besides you're on vacation, relax enjoy yourself. What are you afraid of? Sin takes it back and pulls it again. Sin says; okay looks like Nervius and I are gonna have all the fun. They go back and forth between them until it is all gone. Now getting back to our earlier conversation it's something that is totally different from any other experience you can have. Perfect and Cluey looks at each other and then looks at Sin. Cluey ask, how was it? Sin says, it was great. It is a feeling that is not like anything else to get your body satisfied like that or get it what it desires. Cluey asked desires? What are desires? Sin leans in whispering, she flips up her eye, now girls you are kidding me right? She looks at the blank expressions on their faces. She continues well desires are what your body craves, what your body is curious about what it wants to feel, like someone touching you, to make you feel good, this help your body feel good, less stressed and sadness. Perfect innocently asked; when were you ever stressed or sad? Sin says, well I wasn't really stressed or sadness. But mostly, I was really curious how the two bodies would connect, caressing, touching, feeding the needs of my body is more important to me than a lot of things. Being with a male Theirkind, It is the single greatest, sensation your body will ever experience. I have many desires that my body requires of me every day. Cluey and Perfect looked stunned because they had not tapped into that part of their minds yet. Sin says, some day you will find out what you're missing. Nervius is laying out on his beach chair. Perfect and Nervius share one bamboo umbrella. Perfect looks over at him, he is lying there on his back with his eye closed. Perfect is looking curiously at him from head to toe, thinking about the conversation she, Sin and Cluey just had. She looks at his bare chest, his arms, his legs, the noticeable bulge in his swim trunks, his feet, the shape of his mouth, the rhythm of his breathing, the rise and fall of his chest, she cannot help but notice the large unsightly wound on the side of his face, that goes from the right side of his chin up passed his nose up to the top of his head. He turns his head toward Perfect and she turns her head quickly away, as though not to allow him to catch her looking at him. His head is turned toward her but his eye is closed. She looks over in his direction again and this time their eyes meet, he catches her staring at him. He says, hey why are you looking at me? She replies; I was just curious, He says; curious about what? She slowly replies. About ......the.......wound. She really meant, about Theirkind men in general. It must have been a terrible accident? He turns on his back looking straight up at the grass umbrella. Yes it was. It was quite bad, my folks didn't think I was going to make it, but I did. Perfect asked, is it hard to talk about? Nervius replies; sometimes it is; my best friend was in the car with me, he was killed. That was a lot harder for me to bare, than this scare. But I guess you could say that I was lucky, I survived it. And that was then and this is now. I'm here and that is what counts. Perfect says, I understand, we don't have to talk about it anymore if you don't want to. I'm sorry I was just being nosey. Nervius said, not at all, I've come to realize, you're not the first to inquire about the scare and the accident and you want be the last. The four continued their great time at the beach and return to their rooms to chill out. Perfect, Cluey, and Sin are in their room and Nervius has his own room. But the rooms are next to each other. The three Theirkind women are in their room sitting on their beds when Sin pipes up; hey guys lets hit the town and really party tonight, hit all the popular bars, drink and really celebrate. Perfect says I'm in. Cluey yells; Heeeeyyyy that's cool y'all. I wanna go out and shake til I break it. Then we can go and get some scrimps and chips and get drunk and pass the hell out. Cluey jumps up starts dancing twerking and high fiving Perfect. Sin spins around and pulls Perfect close to her. She says; see that's why I don't want to hang out with her. She's embarrassing. Shake it til I break it? What is she talking about shaking and breaking something and what in the hell are scrimps? Perfect laughs; Sin she's really harmless, that's just the way she is, she doesn't mean anything by it. Sin replies; she is embarrassing as hell. Her parents attend the same country club as my folks do and they are some kinda *special crazy. Her mom is always at the club in hair rollers, drinking, smoking, cursing at her dad. Her dad owns a landscape business, he runs around all day pulling up Sash out of the garden areas, he chops it up, trying to sell it to everybody, then sit's out by the pool smoking it all day trying to block out her crazy mother. That mama that thing is good and crazy. Perfect laughs and says; hey I've known Cluey since grade school, I never said that she wasn't sort of special, but sometimes you've gotta love folks past the good and the bad. Besides she is our friend maybe you need to just give her chance. Sin says; hey I just know her she's your friend crazy thing. They start laughing and throwing pillows, hitting Cluey on the head and soon they were in brawled in a good old fashion pillow fight. Later that night, they're out partying the night away, bar hopping and drinking. Nervius, Perfect, Cluey, and Sin are all seated at the bar the music is blaring. They're dancing in their seats. As they rock their heads to the music all four have had quite a bit to drink. The music stops and a beautiful woman takes the stage. Her name is Temptation she's wearing a tight short fire red sleeveless sexy dress that dips well down into her cleavage area. She has on red fish net stockings supported by pretty red lacy garters. She has long black hair with her full luscious lips painted with bright red lipstick. She starts to sing her seductive song. I miss you baby come and be with me. I got all your desires and fantasies inside of me. Touch me softly and touch me rough. I like it both ways as long as you give me enough. My thighs are soft and quivering just for you. Their slippery and wet they know what you want to do. I got everything you need. I miss you baby come and be with me. You know you need me. She moves down the stairs and slowly through the crowd stopping at each table casting her spell. The men are captivated by her. She's taunting them with her hip. She strokes her hand across their face. She has them under her spell. They start putting money in her garters. Nervius is captivated by her, he says to himself. She would never want me. She has every man in the club under her spell. Just then she reaches the bar, stops right in front of Nervius's stool, he is frozen under her spell, she strokes his face and leans in and kisses him softly on his scarred face. After the show. All of them are partied out. They take shuttles to every stop, until the wee hours in the morning, they finally return to their rooms. Sin pulls out her Sash bag again and lights up. She and Nervius are smoking and she finally convinces an already intoxicated, Perfect to take a drag of her Sash. Cluey refuses she said that she was too scared. Perfect's head spend around. Their resort was the last stop for the shuttle. They all get off, they can barely able to walk. Nervius is so drunk the girls have to guide him to his door, Perfect is sitting on the floor in the hall against the wall in the hotel passed out. Their rooms are side by side. As they lead Nervius into his room Perfect is sitting on the floor until the girls can get their door open. They get Nervius into his room he falls out across the bed mumbling something. They get their door open and pick Perfect up off the floor. Sin laughs and says hey let play a trick on Perfect and Nervius. Cluey asked what kind of trick? Let's put them in bed together, and when they wake up, we will see how funny they'll look, in the morning when they think they have slept with each other. Cluey says, oh Sin you are so bad, I don't think that's a good idea, should we really do that? After all they are our friends. Sin says oh come on Cluey, stop tripping, it's just fun, we're not hurting them, it's just a joke. Cluey finally gives in, they picked Perfect up off the floor, and guides her into the room with Nervius. Sin says; now we have to really make them think, that they did something. I know let's remove their clothes. Cluey gasped; oh Sin I don't think that would be such a good idea. Oh Cluey it's funny, they're both drunk, I mean really what could happen. Cluey said but I'm scared. Sin says what's new you're scared of everything anyway. Cluey gave in, knowing better helps Sin to remove Perfect and Nervius's clothes and laid them side by beside under the covers. They both went to their room. At some point, during the night, both of them being very intoxicated, and very high on Sash, found each other in the bed. The warmth of their bodies makes they embrace. Their lips find each other, kissing, touching every part of each other, caressing, and before long their legs were intertwine, and through their clouded judgments, their bodies make that deep penetrating connection, over and over again, until they are hopelessly lost in the throws, of deep passionate lovemaking. The morning light peers through the window, Cluey and Sin are asleep, midmorning approaches, Cluey awakes and looks at the clock in the room. It's 10:45 am. She calls to Sin and says; hey wake up, Sin turns over in her bed to face Cluey. She yarns while talking, what time is it? It's 10:45, what do you think is going on next door. Do you think they know by now? Sin says, I don't think the volcano has erupted yet? Cluey says; they can't know yet. They are probably still asleep. And they were still asleep. Cluey says, oh Sin what have we done? I'm scared about doing this. Oh girl shut up and take a pill. In the other room, Perfect moves her arm across his face and he flips over in the bed causing the movement of the bed to wake Perfect up. Her head is banging from all the drinking the night before. She's going in and out of sleepiness. She starts to yarn and stretch, her eye opens, she's looking up at the ceiling. She's a little dizzy. She turns toward the window and peers out at the beautiful day awaiting her. Just then she hears this sound in the room a snoring sound, not just in the room but the sound is coming from the lump lying next to her. She says, Cluey turn over you are snoring. The sound then clears its throat. Perfect thinks, this voice is much too deep to be Cluey. She sits up in the bed she's still thinking this is Cluey, they're supposed to be sharing a bed together. She says again Cluey turn over you are snoring. The deep voice says okay. Perfect is confused as to why Cluey would sound that way. She says; very funny Cluey. She reaches for the covers and pulls them back. She belts out a loud scream; Nervius jumps up in the bed what the hell are you doing here? Perfect shouts; what are you doing in my bed! Nervius shouts back; look around you, this is not your bed this is my bed! You missy are in the wrong damn room. How did this happen! Perfect jumps up pulling the covers around her, pulling all of the covers off Nervius us exposing his naked body. She screams again, where are your clothes? Put some clothes on. Nervius snaps; I will if you will give me a chance. He stumbles out of bed falling over to his suite case and quickly pulls a robe from there, to wrap himself up. Perfect said how did this happen? I don't remember anything else after we left the last club last night. Nervius said I don't know what happened here either. I don't remember anything after the last club. How did we end up in bed together? Nervius asked; I don't know. But I have a feeling who's behind it. Nervius asked; Ah did anything happen? Perfect said I think so. We must never tell anyone. Nervius said; I agree it's our secret. Perfect I'm so sorry. Perfect says; no that's okay. It was only my first time. They stand there looking at each other. About that time a knock was at the door. Nervius scrambles over to the door and opens it. There stands Cluey and Sin peeking in holding their mouths hiding their laughter. Nervius said okay so you guys did this. Perfect snaps; (shouting while gripping the covers around her). What a dirty trick, I'm supposed to be your friend, I'm mad at both of you. How could you do such a thing? Sin pipes up; Oh Perfect we were only playing a joke on you guys. You only slept off your drinking together. What is the big deal? Hey let's all get dressed she laughs; well you two get dressed and lets go downstairs to breakfast. So they all met for breakfast and spent the rest of their vacation having fun and soon all returned home to Willowiest.*

2

The Birth

Several months go by, the young Their kinds are deeply focused on their careers. Nervius and Perfect are hanging out, after a long day at work. Perfect says to Nervius; I don't know what's wrong with me. Lately, I've been feeling so weird. I'm hungry all the time and I'm always so sleepy, I just have no energy. I really just feel strange. Nervius laughs; that's because you are strange. Perfect snaps at him; oh shut up Nervius. He replies; don't be so touchy, I'm only kidding. It's probably a bug or something. Or maybe you're just tired from all the studying we did to graduate, and then turning around and really pushing yourself with the new job. I know it's been that way for me too. Perfect replies; yeah you're probably right. But to be on the safe side, I did make a doctor's appointment today, just to make sure everything is all right. Would you mind going with me? Nervius responds; sure I'll go with you. Perfect says; good thanks I could use the moral support, but first I need to stop off by my place so I can change clothes. For some reason this skirt feels so tight today. So off they went to Perfects house. They go in Perfect says; come on in and have a seat, I want be long. Nervius comes in and takes a seat and waits patiently for her in the living room. She goes into the bedroom to change her clothes. Perfect starts to undress, when a strong unfamiliar pain cuts through her back. She bends over, grabbing her back with one hand. She holds on to the bed post with the other hand. The pain quickly subsides. She says to herself; what the what was that? She pauses for a moment, regains her composure and continues changing. About two minutes later, another powerful pain cuts through her belly. This time it takes her to the floor. She screams out to Nervius. Nervius! Come quick help me! Nervius jumps to his feet and comes rushing into the room. He looks around for her. Perfect yelps; over here quick, I need you!!! He sees her crumpled on the floor he quickly rushes to her side. He says; let me help you up, he tries to move her. She screams no don't move me. I.........I don't know what's wrong with me. Nervius shouts; I'll go get help! She screams in pain again no! no! Don't leave me please. Hold my hand! Maybe if I lay steel it will go away. He holds her hand he looks terrified. Nervius is trying to comfort her as she lies on the floor quivering in pain, she puts her knees up, and she feels something rumbling inside of her body. Not understand what was going on inside of her, she tries to lay very steel on the floor hoping the pain would pass, but it doesn't. She give a loud scream with a tremendous urge to push something from her body. She's sweating profusely, she bares down gives a big push, nothing happens, she feels the urge to push again, she's almost breaking Nervius's hand, she bares down and something tremendously warm and wet emerges from her body, filling her underwear pushing them down her legs. She feels under her skirt, it's a wet and warm blob. Nervius looks between her legs where the blob is and almost passes out. Perfect said what is it? Nervius is on his knees at her feet in shock. Nervius says; I don't know I think it's a blob with a baby in it. Perfect props herself upon her elbows, a baby OMG. She feels down to where the blob is and feels a tiny little body moving right beneath her. She quickly tells Nervius to go and get some towels from the linen closet. He's frozen still at her feet. She shouts; Now Nervius quickly! Nervius rushes to get some towels from the linen closet, he quickly returns to her side. She retrieves the wet baby out of her under ware, from between her legs, puts it on her chest, and starts to it clean up. This baby is starring at them with one eye. It's a cute little one eyed Their kind baby boy

They both are starring at the baby and in that moment, something most alarming and unexpected happens. The other side of the baby's face lights up, it's another eye, the baby has two eyes and it's starring back at Perfect and Nervius. Perfect and Nervius stares in horror. The baby was born a Two Eyed Their kind. Suddenly, Nervius shouts; oh crap Perfect! It has two eyes.....that means......you've been with a two eyes. How could you let this happen? Perfect snaps back; what do you mean how could I let this happen? I don't know how it happened it just came out with two eyes. You were my first and only. Perfect has the baby wrapped in a towel. Nervius lifts her up off the floor onto the bed with the baby in her arms. She is now resting against some pillows. Nervius asked; how do you feel? She replies; very tired but a lot better now. She stares at her baby sleeping in her arms. She's looking at the baby smiling all that pain for this little one to come into the world. Nervius states; Perfect you are a one eye, I am a one eye. How could this be possible? Perfect responds; well you are the only one I have ever been with. This is your child as well. Nervius snaps; no it is not! You know it's against the law to inbreed. You can be arrested for this. You know you cannot keep this child. Perfect responds; well I am going to keep it. This is our child and I don't care about the law, inbreeding, or him having two eyes. Nervius tries to reason with her. Perfect you know this child will never be accepted among our kind. Perfect responds; well they don't have to accept it I had it and I love it. Nervius says; do you know what you're getting yourself into? Perfect says; Nervius yes I do. That means we have a child together and I'm going to take care of this, so stop asking me so many stupid questions. And another thing you have to promise me that you will never tell anyone. Nervius looks at her; okay I promise I want say anything, but you're crazy. I know what we can do, let's kill it no one will know. Perfect screams at him; you idiot get away from me, you are crazy? I would never do that. Nervius says; Perfect I'm sorry, but you are crazy to think that you can get away with this. I'm just trying to help. I know what we can do. Let's put out one of its eye's. Perfect shouts; you dumb azz! Do you think I would let you hurt my baby? Nervius says; Perfect I was only making some suggestions to you. But you'd better figure this out quick, before someone see's you with this baby or the council catches you. Perfect rocking her baby; it's obvious, that you don't want anything to do with our baby. But since you are partially responsible for all of this, you could at least help me out until I can get back on my feet. I have to find a place for the baby. Someone who will take good care of him. Now help me clean up this mess. No one can never know that this happened here. Now take everything out back and burn it. Perfect takes a month's leave to recover from her well-kept secret. She decides to hide the child out in the west side of the island in a two eyed community, with a two eyed care giver named Marley. She's well known among the Two eyed community who takes care of children. Especially secret special children. Marley is a kind, patient, spiritual two eyed middle age Their kind, she is a pillar of strength for many and her home is a refuge to many secrets that is among all Their kinds on the island. Perfect visits her baby every day for the next 3 months, bringing things over to aide in the care for her son. Marely is doing a fantastic job taking care of the tiny Their kind. Perfect: (Knocking on the door while watching behind her) MARLEY: Hi please come in. Perfect: How's my baby doing? Marley (Smiling) the baby is fine. Have you told the father of your child? Perfect; He knows but he wants nothing to do with the child. He' a one eye so he's denying the child is his. Marley (Looking shocked) He's a one eye? The father of this child is a one eye? Are you absolutely sure? Perfect; (begins to cry) Yes Marley I'm sure. You sound like my child's father. Of course I'm sure. He was the only one. My baby doesn't deserve any of this. I don't know what I'm going to do. Marley said; come sit down. Ms. Perfect think about this. How could a Two Eyed baby be born to two one eyed parents? Something is wrong here. You know that this is impossible. Perfect is weeping; I know it sounds crazy and I don't understand either, but this is the child that came out of my body. I had the baby at home so I know that he is mine. Marley says; dear this is a mystery right now but I know it is more behind this. But Perfect the child is find here with me. Perfect (drying her tears she snaps) this isn't right! I should be taking care of my child not you! Marley I don't know what I'm going to do. All I know is that I love my child and all I want is the best for him. I know he is different and there is a great chance my parents will not accept him. It's really difficult to see what someone else is going through until it happens to you that's when you know their struggles. But after all they are my parents and they're supposed to love me, they will have to understand. I have nowhere else to turn.(Perfect picking up her child from his crib, embracing the child in her arms) My beautiful baby with an imperfect face. She plants a soft kiss on the baby's forehead and rocks the baby slowly then places him back down in his crib. She asks; Marley have you ever had someone to come into your life that you didn't expect, you came to love them, and you shared time that you really didn't know would be that short and then before you know it you were apart from them and you felt like because of the circumstances, you never got a chance to make it the best of that situation with them. Marley says; Perfect come and sit down. They both took a seat in the living room. Marley began, yes I do know what it is like to love someone and suddenly their not with me. Not long ago I was married. Perfect stares at her, as the sadness moves surrounds her aurora. I was married briefly. My husband was as full of life as anyone could be. Marley looks up as she continues speaking. His personality alone would fill a room for the evening. We dated a long time. Too long I think. He wanted to marry me 6 months after we met and I would not allow it because I felt that we didn't know each other long enough. He did sculptures for a living and was extraordinarily talented. He was a dreamer and we often set around planning our future and how we'd buy and RV and travel the island selling his work. He had to keep a basic job to help meet the bills but he was a vision and a force of all of his own and I loved him for that. Perfect asked: If you don't mind me asking. So what happened? Where is he now? Marley replied, well at the end of a 3 year relationship we decided finally to get married. We had a beautiful wedding actually my first wedding. We kept it very simple only 60 people attended. Leading up to the wedding early fall, he became ill, but bless his heart he wanted to have the wedding and go on our honeymoon so we did. Immediately after we returned he and was hospitalized. He fought hard and I fought hard to save him. He died forty days after our wedding. Perfect gasped covering her mouth, whispering I'm so sorry. I remember noticing the box of wedding items stacked in a box, sitting at the foot of the bed that I had not had an opportunity to go through yet. And along beside it was the black leather binder that they gave me from the funeral home. There was the evidence of my life in that moment in a nutshell. That changed my life forever. Ms. Perfect time waits for no one. Don't waste time. Tears were meeting under Marley's cheeks. Perfect got up from where she was seated with tears in her eye and walked over to where Marley was and did what was forbidden according to the law between a one eye and a two eyes, she embraced Marley. Marley I am so sorry for your lost that must have been devastating for you to go through. Marley replied yes it was but what we sometimes go through can be for other people as much as it can be for us. With Yahweh's help I am stronger now. Perfect stands back and looks at her Yahweh? Marley yes He is my strength, my rock, my light, my everything. Perfect sarcastically responds, okay alrighty. Marley changes the subject. Now Ms. Perfect please do not feel like you are the only one with a secret on this island. Because there are many out there. But you must think with caution and reason. You will not be able to keep this child a secret forever. And I would not advise you to reveal the child to your parents. Your father isn't he part of the council for willowiest? Perfect responds; yes he is, why do you bring that up? I don't need you to advise me on anything. Marley replies; the council is very firm about the laws they make. And you father has taken certain vows as a council member to uphold those laws and the consequences of those who break them. Perfect snaps at her; well I guess I will just have to make them except my baby for who he is. I will make they understand. Marley (Marley nods her head) as you please Ms. Perfect. Perfect soon departs Marley's house she goes home. A month later Perfect is at home in her bed and she's so exhausted she falls into a deep sleep. She started to dream she was in a field the wind was blowing, the fields had tall yellow wheat grass that was swaying back and forth, in the wind and she heard herself laughing. The sun was extremely bright, there was a glow of light she had never seen before. She hears a voice in the distance, it was Nervius he was smiling running toward her and in his arms was their baby and as they met their baby lifted up from his arms and was hovering just above them, they were so happy, they ran among this wheat fields, dancing and playing, the three of them were finally a family and they danced and played throughout the field. Her parents were there and all was well. Sweet music was playing and bells were ringing and long after the music stopped the bells kept ringing and ringing and the ringing kept getting louder and louder until the noise awakened her. It was her phone ringing, she grabs the phone, and her heart is beating fast, she's panting from her fantasy dream. She answers; hello Marley, Hi Perfect its Marley. (Marley can hear her panting on the other end of the phone)Marley: Hello Perfect are you okay? Perfect answers; Hi I just woke up I'm okay Marley replies; Good that's good ....Ah Perfect I need to talk to you about something. Could you come over today? Perfect responses: Wait a minute talk to me about what? Marley: (takes a deep breath) it's about the baby. Perfect snaps back; what's wrong? Is there something wrong with my baby? What is it? Marley: Nothing Perfect the child is fine I just need to talk to you. I would rather speak with you in person. Can you come over today? Perfect: Yes I'll be there this afternoon. Marley: Good I'll see you then. They hang up.

3

The Visit

Perfect arrives at Marley's house in minutes as promised. She's still very nervous as to what Marley is going to say to her. She rings the doorbell. Marley opens the door and immediately invites her in. They take a seat on the couch. Perfect says; I want to see my baby right now! Can you please go and get him and bring him to me. Marley say's; yes I will but first I must talk with you. I need to explain some things to you that you don't know about the child. Perfect cuts her off. No you can't explain anything to me until you go and get my child and I lay my eye on him. Marley stops her conversation and goes to get the baby. As Marley is walking away, she can hear Perfect is still fussing to herself. What do you mean things I don't know about my baby. Marley soon returns to the room but she's empty hand-ed. What happens next will take Perfect by total surprise. Entering the room directly behind Marley is a little glowing light floating across the room. It's Perfect's baby suspended in midair smiling and cooing following Marley into the room. Perfect almost faints. Marley retakes her seat on the couch beside Perfect. Perfect's mouth is open is if she will never close it again. Marley speaks to her. Ms. Perfect this is what I wanted to speak to you about. Before you actually saw it. Perfect finally manage to say something. What happened to my baby? Marley replies; nothing has happened to you baby that wasn't time to happen to your baby. I need to ex-plain something to you. Perfect looks at Marley, then looks at her baby, and then looks back at Marley and says you can ex-plain this? Marley replies, yes I can. Perfect says again, OMG what's happened to my baby? Marley replies; Nothing has happened to him. See the baby's abilities are a result of the next dimension spiritual realm. This is why the councilman of Willowiest has forbidden the mixing of the different spe-cies. Because it creates a power of a spiritual presence. That they can't control. So they fear it because they don't under-stand it. It is more powerful than all the power they think money gives them. They label it as witchcraft and voodoo and it is not. They have brainwashed everyone in to believing the worst. Perfect asked; so what you're telling me is, that my baby, is one of a kind? Marley well he is unique but not one of a kind. He can fly, he glows, and he has the ability to heal. As I care for them they cares for me. Perfect asked; them?

Them what them. Are there more? Marley gets up from the couch and motions for Perfect to follow her to another back bedroom. There she opens another bedroom door and there are two more babies floating in midair. Marley says; Perfect I would like for you to meet Grace and Favor they are your baby's playmates. Perfect's eye grew wide. Wow there are three of them. Perfect looks on in disbelief. One has Three eye's Marley says yes that's Grace she is a little girl, she has the same abilities as your baby. Perfect says, and the other one is Favor he has four eyes. Marley says that he has the same abilities and maybe more. They came to me shortly after they were born. Actually the same month as your little one did. I'm very concerned about the mothers, they told me that they did not know when they would be back because they were being watched. Perfect asked, by whom? They did not say. I hope they are okay, I haven't heard from their mothers in all this time. Marley closes the door and they return to the living room and take their seats again. Perfect's baby comes over and lands gently on he's mother's lap. PERFECT LOOKS AT HER BABY AND EMBRACES HIM TENDERLY IN HER ARMS, TEARS ARE SCREAMING DOWN HER FACE, SHE FEELS THE WARMTH OF THE LOVING GLOW FROM HIS TINY BODY. THE LIGHT AROUND HIM IS A PERFECT PEACE. SHE NOTICES A BANDAIDE ON HER INDEX FINGER WHERE SHE CUT HERSELF WITH A KITCHEN KNIFE A FEW DAYS AGO. SHE REMOVES THE BANDAIDE AND THE CUT HAD DISAPEARS BEFORE HER EYE. TEARS ARE ROLLING DOWN HER FACE SHE PLACES A GENTLE

KISS ON HER BABY'S FOREHEARD. WHILE LOOKING AT HER BABY SHE SAYS; YOU KNOW MARLEY I HAVEN'T EVEN GIVEN HIM A NAME. MARLEY REPLIES; SO HAVE YOU THOUGHT OF ONE YOU HAVE IN MIND. SHE LOOKS AT HIM AND SAID, I THINK I WILL CALL HIM MERCY, BECAUSE HIS LITTLE LIFE DESERVES ALL THE MERCY THIS WORLD WILL GIVE HIM. MARLEY SMILES AND SAYS; MS, PERFECT I THINK THAT IS A WONDERFUL NAME FOR HIM. PERFECT LOOKS AT HER BABY AND SAYS; YOUR NAME IS MERCY AND YOUR MOMMY LOVES YOU SO MUCH. SHE TURNS TO MARLEY AND SAYS; YOU HAVE SHOWN ME SOMETHING TODAY ABOUT MY BABY, THAT I COULD NOT HAVE EVER IMAGINED IN MY LIFETIME. AND AT ALL COST, I HAVE TO FIGURE OUT WHAT I HAVE TO DO TO PROTECT HIM. PERFECT STANDS UP KISSES HER BABY AND SAYS MY PERCIOUS LITTLE ONE, MOMMY HAS TO GO NOW AND MAKE PLANS TO PROTECT YOU. SHE LOOKS AT MARLEY. PERFECT SAYS, I GUESS ALL MY LIFE I TRULY HAVE BEEN PREVILLIAGE I 'VE NEVER HAD TO DEAL WITH BIGOTRY MARLEY RESPSONDS; MS. PERFECT NO ONE WINS NOT THE HATERS OR THE HATED. . YOU CAN NO MORE ASKED OF ANYONE WITH A CLOSED MIND TO UNDERSTAND DIFFERENCE, THAN YOU CAN ASKED OF A BLIND MAN TO GASE UPON THE HORIZON, FOR HE IS BLIND, HE WILL NEVER SEE.

THEY DRINK ALL THE POSION AND THEN WAIT ON US TO DIE. PERFECT ASKED; POISION. MARLEY REPLIES; YES THE POSION OF CORRUPTION, WARS, AND SCANDALS. OUR GRAVEYARDS ARE VERY OLD AND ARE FEW THEIR GRAVEYARDS ARE WITH MANY AND ARE FULL. BEFORE THINGS GET TO BAD. PLEASE LOOK AT ALL POSSIBILITIES IN MOVING THE BABIES TO A SAFER PLACE. PERFECT PROMISE MARLEY THAT SHE WILL. SHE LEAVES AND MARLEY TAKES MERCY BACK TO HIS ROOM. MERCY LIFT OFF MARLEY'S HANDS AND STARTS BACK DOWN THE HALL TO HIS ROOM. PERFECT DRIVES AWAY FROM MARLEY'S HOME STILL IN TOTAL SHOCK BECAUSE SHE REACHES HOME COMES IN AND COLLASPE ON HER BED. LYING THERE SHE'S STARRING INTO SPACE (ABOUT THAT TIME NERVIUS CALLS PERFECT AND SHE ANSWERS. (She hears her phone ringing she picks it up but does not speak into it) NERVIUS: Hello........ Perfect..... Are you there? HEY WHAT'S GOING ON WITH YOU? PERFECT!!....Are you there? HELLO? (She snaps out of her trans and answers him) PERFECT: I'M.........I'M......... HERE... NERVIUS: WELL YOU DON'T SOUND GOOD..... (LOOKING AROUND WHISPERING INTO THE PHONE) IS EVERYTHING OKAY WITH YOU KNOW WHAT? PERFECT does not answer him..... NERVIUS: HEY what's going on with you are you there? Talk to me. PERFECT finally speaks: I'm here I'm sorry ....I guess I'm a little distracted but everything is fine.

Nervius: (Whispering) and your situation? Perfect: Everything is good. Nervius S: hey I was calling to ask if you would like to meet for dinner tonight at the club in town. You know to maybe talk this over. Perfect replies; ah that's fine but I think I'm going to take a nap first and I'll give you a call when I wake up. Nervius says; okay and they hang up. Perfect; (Thinking to herself): how could this have happened to me? Why did this happen? My child has two eyes, he flies through the air, and he can heal. Just then her phone beeps, it's a text from Nervius. Nervius: Hey don't mean to bother u, just concerned,   checking on you again. You sounded so weird earlier. Perfect replies back; k Nervius text I take it u don't really feel up to going anywhere later on do you? Perfect; replies No not really I have a lot to think about. Nervius types you mean about him. Perfect types; Yes him and he now has a name. Nervius types; really and what would that be. Perfect types; Mercy Nervius types; Mercy what kind of name is that and why wasn't I included in this? Perfect types; you don't want anything to do with him so you are an absent tee father so I did what I had to do. Nervius writes; that name sounds weak. Perfect types; oh how dare you. IT'S NOT A WEAK NAME YOU MAGGOTT NUTT. IT MEANS TO SHOW COMPASSION. Not to mention the fact that he's been alive for almost 6 months and you have not even tried to see him. Don't try and tell me what to name my child. Our child! Nervius types; okay okay I'm sorry stop getting so upset. Nervius writes; Per you know I'm just not there yet I need some time. Perfect wrote; Fine do what cowards do best run. Stop texting me I'm tired. Then texting finally stops between them because it was only getting more intense. Perfect is busy around the house the next morning cleaning her house, she comes across some toys in a bag that she bought for Mercy. She gets and idea she says to herself I know an outing that will be good for the baby and me. Just some time along. She gets dressed and heads for Marley's house.

4

Shopping Trip

erfect shows up unannounced at Marley's house Marley opens the door for her Marley opens the door with a big smile; Hi Ms. Perfect come on in you're here early Mercy will be happy to see you. Perfect replies with a smug look on her face; Marley, I'm taking my baby shopping. Marley (cautiously speaking); Perfect........ Do you think it would be wise to take the child out? Don't you think that seems a little risky? Perfect snaps: Well who else does he have? Besides I 'm not asking for your advice or your permission to take my baby anywhere!!I know my child thank you, we will be fine...... (Snapping again) And he is my child anyway!!.... ....I can do whatever I well please with him!!! Marley (BOWING HER HEARD) as you wish Ms. Perfect......Perfect: In fact.........give me his clothing we are going for the day ......he's six months old and it's time to get him out of this jail. Marley says; sure.......whatever you say.....Marley hands her the baby bag and opens the door for her and the child. Perfect maneuvers the stroller out of the door and in moments their out of sight. Perfect takes the young Their kind child out for a stole. They go shopping and the tiny Their kind sleeps through the shopping adventure. She goes to the market the baby continues to sleep. She goes to the movies the baby continues to sleep. She starts back to Marley's house when she is spotted by her friends Sin and Cluey, they approach her quickly. Perfect is startled by their fast approach. Sin is waving her hand in the air; Perfect!!.......... Hey.......... Perfect!!.........wait...........over here. (Perfect wants to die in that moment she approaches them slowly. Cluey says; Well........ Well....... what do we have here? Perfect says; (Very nervously) oh nothing really? Sin asked; whose baby is that in the stroller? Because I know you don't have a child. Perfect says; Well.......I'm...Ah...I'm... keeping this little one for a friend. Cluey says; Oh snap how sweet. Whose child is this? Perfect replies; A friend......you don't know them. Sin asked; who? I know everyone on the island and I don't remember anyone who just had a baby. Perfect: Well you don't know them. And I've got to go now. Cluey ask; hey let me take a look I wanna see if it's ugly or not. Perfect: Noooo!!!! Nooo!!! You can't its sleeping. Cluey says; girl I ain't gone wake it up....quit tripping. Perfect starts backing away from them. She turns the stroller around and starts running away from them. Sin yells; hey wait Perfect wait a minute. Cluey says; girl let her go it's probably ugly as hell anyway that's way she's dodging everybody. Perfect yelling back; No no.....not now......gotta go sorry!!! ....you guys I really have to run have to get the baby back to its mother...I promise we'll do something soon......sorry gotta run!! (She thought of anything quickly to say so she could make her escape) Perfect was out of sight in moments. Out of breath thinking to herself Whew... that was a close call. I thought I could do this.....this is my child I shouldn't be afraid of showing him to anyone....but I can't help wondering what will they think of him? And I shouldn't care. But what will they think of me? How can I take him home to my parents? What will they think of him? What will they think of me? I shouldn't care what anyone thinks I am a proud rich One eyed Theirkind I'm an elitist, why should I care what they think, Wow this mothering thing is hard, and I'm so tired from just running away from Sin and Cluey. I have to get something to eat. But the problem was she did care. She spots a lunch deli across the street and she crosses over to go inside and get some lunch. The baby is still asleep she parks the stroller outside and goes inside to get a bite to eat. Inside: The clerk waits on her; Good afternoon Madame. What can I get for you today? Perfect: Well let's see. I'm so hungry. I'll have a mulberry croissant with deli cheese and a spritzer to go. She's paying for her items when she hears a commotion going on right outside the deli. Theirkinds are gathering and pointing and talking......Reaching for her bag, Perfect turns to see what all the noise is about. As she walks toward the door, she sees what all the attention is about, her body goes completely limp. Her eye could not believe what it was seeing. She dropped her purchases on the floor and ran out of the shop. There suspended in midair was a little blue blanket hovering about 3 feet above the stroller. The baby was awake. Perfect trembling and trying not to panic gently pulls the blanket back down inside the stroller. And folks began asking her questions. Passer byer: How did you do that? Is there really a baby in there or is it a balloon? Passer byer 2: what kind of blanket floats in the air by itself? Perfect had to come up with something quick the baby had drawn to much attention to them. Perfect responds smiling; it's a...........a....... magic trick with wires...that's....that's right............... you just can't see the wires. (Laughing nervously) Well the show is over folks that will be all for today. She speeds away again. Perfect is on her way back to Marley's house when she runs into a disturbance on the street. It's two One eyed Theirkinds fighting. Their throwing things breaking windows the police show up and break up the fight. The police says the store owner's property has been damaged. You all know the law pay for it now or its two days in jail. The two One eye's that were fighting are now arguing. He started it. No he started it. They both said we're not paying for it. We will take two days in jail. But the Willowiest law states the One eyes cannot be locked up no matter what laws they break. And that Two eyes and Three eyes can be taken into custody in their place to do the time for the One eyes. A bus pulls up and the police boards the bus and pulls a Two eye's and Three eye's off the bus and arrest them to do the time in jail for the One eye's that were fighting. Some of the young One eyes that were in the crowd became furious because they saw the laws as ridiculous and outdated. One young One eyes called another one and said hey we must do something I just witnessed two friends of mine, arrested for no reason, and sent to jail to cover the wrong doing of two One eyes fighting and destroying property. This is an injustice and it must stop. Tonight we must have an emergency meeting. The voice on the other end of the phone agreed. Hey they can't keep locking up innocent Theirkinds. Well tonight we need to have an emergency meeting. To plan a course of acting against these crazy laws.

BACK AT MARLEYS HOUSE

Marley opens the door. Perfect parks the stroller in the living room and takes a seat at the kitchen table. Marley: HI...... how was your outing? Perfect: interesting? Marley: Only interesting? Perfect explains; (with her hand on her forehead) Marley the baby was floating in midair today outside on the street! Marley states; Ms. Perfect you knew he could fly and that he glows. Perfect snaps; well you should have tried harder to convince me not to go. I almost passed out today when he was floating over the stroller and peeking out from under the blanket at me. Marley says; I did tell you everything about him. You did not listen. Perfect still snapping; Watch you tone with me. I am still your employer. Marley says; yes Ms. Perfect... Perfect says; I have had a nerve racking day I have to go now. Marley says; I know Ms. Perfect it must have been quite a challenging day for you. One thing did you change the baby? Perfect looks puzzled; ah change the baby what do you mean? Marley explains; baby Theirkinds have to be changed and fed at least three times a day. That's probably why he woke up. Perfect snaps; you never explained that to me! Marley responds; when you left you said that you knew all you needed to know. Now the child is quiet wet. But it's all right I will take care of it. And I will feed him. He is a good baby he never cries just smiles and plays. Will you be by tomorrow? Perfect looks sad; I'll be by tomorrow I guess I really suck at this mothering thing don't I? Marley says; Ms. Perfect this was your first outing with the baby, it's all new right now, and it's a lot to learn about these little ones. Perfect responds; Marley thank you for not judging me and I'm sorry about how I acted earlier. Marley replies; that's okay apology accepted. Perfect kisses her baby good bye and leaves Marley's house confused, exhausted, and weary. Marley tucked the babies in and decided to turn in herself. But unknowingly to Marley, Mercy was not asleep, he thought about today's events. He got up from his little bed and went over to the window. He was curious about the outdoors, since his mother had taken him out earlier in the day. He went to the cribs, where Grace and Favor were asleep. He woke them up and led them to the window and they set at the window looking at the cars go by and the neighboring houses and buildings in the distance. For the first time they were curious about the outside. They floated to the top near the ceiling where there was a small vent window open. They wiggled their little bodies through the window and was outside the house. They were flying first over the trees and then around the yard. They looked around at the other houses very similar to the one that they lived in. But out in the distance was larger buildings which they were very curious to explore. So they took off. Toward the pretty bright buildings in the distance. It was as if a force of some kind was driving them forward. The first building they came to had a pretty water fountain in front of it. That fascinated them. They began looking in all the windows in the building. They were at the one eye's Prestige University fraternity campus. They entered the building through an open door. It was 3am and everyone was asleep. They giggled at the sounds coming from the frat brothers rooms, as a symphony of snoring filled the halls. They landed on some of their heads just to hear them snore. Their little bodies were illuminating as they sat on different ones heads. They went from room to room, lighting on them one after the other. Giggling at the sounds they made. Although there were no physical ailments going on with the young Theirkind men. A healing took place. Through Grace, Mercy, and Favor their minds were revolutionized. The babies finally grew tired from all of their exploring of the great building and they decided to head for home. They made it back to Marley's house and entered back through the same window where they made their escape. They tucked themselves back in their beds and went to sleep.

5

Nervius's Visit

Perfect awakens in her bed. The stress of her life settles in over her. She feels so alone in her situation. She doesn't know what she will do and she can trust no one with her secret. She's thinking out loud. I didn't make this baby by myself. This baby has a father. Why should I bare this struggle alone? She picks up her phone and punch's up Nervius phone number. She is hesitant to push the call button, but she does. Nervius answers, Hi Perfect what's up? Not much. Question I was just wondering when you were planning to go to see our son. Nervius response slowly honestly I had not plan too just yet. You know Nervius he has two eyes he's not a deadly disease. Perfect you're just going to called me up and dropped this visit stuff on me. Perfect snaps at him but he is your son who's been alive for six months. I would think you'd want to at least want to see him! You don't even care!! I have no one to turn too!! She burst into tears I haven't asked you for anything. And the least you could do is come and see your son. I can't do this by myself any longer, I need your help. Perfect come on please don't cry. Don't cry. You know neither one of us planned this? And we weren't ready for this. Come on babe please stop crying. I'll come and see him. I mean I know what we did but Per this is hard for me too. I just don't know if I'm ready for this. Perfect wiping her tears well when I became a mother whether I liked it or not I had to be ready on day one. So when are you coming by? I've got to work to-morrow but I will be there day after tomorrow. You promise I promise. Perfect feels a little better. Okay I will text you the address and I will meet you there. Okay see you then. Okay good bye good bye. They hang up. Nervius is looking in the mirror, talking to himself rubbing his scared face. That kid ain't ever going to be my son. I don't care how much she tries to convince me. I ain't claiming no two eyed Theirkind as mine. Two days later Perfect and Nervius meet at Marley's house. Nervius standing there nervously wring-ing his hands. Perfect: walks up well hi there glad you came. Nervius: I said that I would. Hey Perfect let's get this over with before I change my mind. Perfect immediately starts ringing the doorbell. Marley answers the door smiling. Marley says: Hello you two please came in. Perfect intro-duces Nervius. Perfect: Marley I would like for you to meet

Nervius. He is Mercy's father. Marley: (Smiling shaking his hand) Oh it is very nice to finally meet you. Nervius says; likewise ah where is the kid I have another pressing appointment to go to? Perfect says: (Perfect rolls her eye at him) Okay Marley will you bring Mercy out so he can see his father. Sure Ms. Perfect I will be right back. Marley disappears in to the back room and in a couple of minutes she emerges from the back room with a small bundle in a blanket. He is still asleep baby Theirkinds sleep a lot in the first year of life. Perfect takes the baby from Marley. She walks toward Nervius with the bundle and he starts backing away saying "hey wait a minute I'll look at him.....but.....but don't think I'm ready for too much else. Perfect: Nervius come down it....is....just....a ...baby Nervius: Okay.......okay......but I don't want to touch it or anything.....How can you come all the way over here and not hold your own son.... you make me sick......you.....you.....slug.......stop! Nervius: Stop! Calling me that......Perfect says; at least look at him.....he's sleeping.....Nervius; why is he asleep? That's what babies do they sleep a lot their first year of life. As Perfect is standing before Nervius holding the small bundled, the blanket starts to move. The baby wakes up. Marley's voice changes into a gentle sweet tone. Marley: Oh hi there little one, you have visitors. Did you enjoy your nap? Oh look at your little smiley face all fresh and ready to play. The little Theirkind is fully awake and ready for play.

Marley walks over to where Perfect is standing holding the young child. Nervius is standing there frozen starring in disbelief. Marley says to Nervius he's quiet gentle, he want hurt you, this is nonsense, you have to hold your son before you leave today it want hurt a bit. Nervius looked frighten and unsure. I.....I don't know......I'm not comfortable with this I don't think I'm ready. Perfect pipes up.....Oh Nervius get a grip on yourself and hold your son. Nervius looks over in the blankets, at the tiny Their Kind starring back at him, and Mercy gives him a big delightful smile. Somehow the baby's smile calmed him down. Perfect says; put out your arms. Nervius gives in to the pressure of Marley and Perfect, he takes a hard swallow, and puts his shaking hands out to take the baby. Perfect gently places the small bundle in his arms. The baby immediately starts cooing and smiling at his father. Nervius stares interestingly into the eyes of the small child. Almost hypnotized; Perfect pipes up and says; go ahead and say something to him let him know you are here to see him. Nervius says with a shaky voice.......AHH ....AHH... it's so small and very warm. The energy starts to flow from the baby onto Nervius. Nervius says: Is it just me or is It getting warm in here. Marley says it's the baby he stays extra warm. Nervius continues holding his son and it begins to get warmer. He stares at the warm bundle moving within his arms, cooing and flirting with him. As he holds the bundle he begins to feel different, like something is changing. He begins to feel lighter. Holding the child in one hand he tugs at his shirt collar with the other. The baby starts to glow a loving glow. Nervius says nothing because the light is so peaceful. He's paralyzed, with his eye fixed on the child. And there is a change occurring with him. The rigidness of the scare on his face starts to change. The scare on his face begins to gets a little smoother. Throughout this process Perfect is watching astonished and cautiously, as a transformation of the father of her child is taking place. Nervius is now sweating profusely. And now the scare is no longer rigid but really smooth and barely visible and fading more. The scare has flatten completely, the skin where the scare use to be is discolored now, light but also changing to his natural shade, and then suddenly where his scare use to be is smooth skin, his natural color has returned. And what happens next would take everyone that's present by total surprise, that now smooth side where the scar healed so well, now there is just an empty side with perfect skin, a slit forms and opens up. Another eye appears. Perfect let's out a scream; oh my goodness! There standing before Perfect, is Nervius fully transformed, into now Nervius a Two eyed Theirkind. Perfect is walking around him, her hand is covering her mouth that she cannot close in disbelief. She says, what in the world just happened to you? Nervius says what do you mean? He's standing there blinking both eyes at her. Perfect: You just grew another eye. Nervius: Perfect that's not funny stop playing with me. Perfect: I'm not playing with you go to the mirror and see for yourself. Nervius hands the baby back to Perfect, and quickly heads over to the mirror. Nervius sees himself for the first time as a two eyes and almost faints. He shouts; what the Sam Mary????!!! What is going on here? Perfect is shouting at Nervius. You have turned into a Two eyes. Nervius response; What do you mean? I am a One Eye.....this is witch craft. That kid has put a spell on me. Perfect says; there are no spells, this explains everything, you have been passing for a One Eye all this time you liar, haven't you? Nervius; Perfect no I haven't. Perfect stares at him in disbelief. What is going on here? You lying slug farker. You were a Two eyes all long. Nervius says; No that's not true. Perfect snaps at him; And to think you looked down our baby like he wasn't nothing. Mercy was born a Two eyes because his father is a Two eyes. Nervius: But.....I......I......am a One Eye.....that's all I remember....Perfect: This all makes sense now. (Nervius totally confused looks at "Perfect) Nervius: what happened? Perfect; our child is very special he is has special powers. This is not witch craft. Our child has the ability to heal so when you held him, he healed your face which revealed your true identity. Nervius turns from the mirror facing Perfect and said. Then who am I? Who shall I be now? This has ruined my life as a One Eyes. I know no other life. Perfect asked him; Tell me Nervius so who were you before the accident. Nervius responds; I don't know.....no ..... I don't remember anything before the accident. Perfect this is all your fault. If you had never brought me here to see this thing it would not have turned me into a Two Eyes. Perfect snaps back; he's not a thing! You nut case. This is your fault for deceiving me and everyone else. Nervius says; you and this thing has ruined my life. I will get you for this Perfect. Marley speaks up: You two please stop arguing neither of you are at fault. This was just a chain of events that was destined to take place. Nervius the child only revealed what was already there. Apparently, you lost your memory and your other eye after the accident. Nervius still very upset in shock storms out of the door.

Marley goes behind him. Perfect stops her and says; let him go. He will be alright, Perfect turns her attention to Mercy. She's smiling at her baby saying my dear one. He will cool down. You are my special little one. Marley turns to her and says. Sweetheart within these walls holds many secrets in our world but not only are they secrets but miraculous mysteries in our time. They are not some unfortunate mishaps. They are fortunate occurrences and they will play an essential part in fulfilling the spiritual purpose for why they were born. And when the revolution come this will make everything better for all of us. Perfect says; here you go Marley with all this revolutionary spiritual mumbo jumbo stuff again. Marley continues; Perfect you must listen to me and listen well. We can never prepare for life, that's already prepared us. Our destiny has been written. Perfect asks; so you mean everything that is happening to me was planned. Marley replies; yes absolutely and never for bad but for the good. That is the beginning of seeing things in the spiritual realm and not the physical. There are accidents but never any mistakes. Perfect looks at her and says; wow all of this is too deep for me right now. I think I'd better go home and get some rest. I'll think about this some more tomorrow. Marley smiles at her and shows her to the door and they say goodnight.

6

Call From Cluey

Perfect is at home, lying on her bed, she is still reeling after the events of the evening. When she gets a call from her friend Cluey. She's crying and screaming into the phone. Perfect's jerk reaction, she sits straight up in her bed. Yelling into the phone. Cluey what's the matter? Cluey doesn't answer she's crying out of control, Perfect says: Cluey calm down please tell me what's going on? What's wrong? Cluey talk to me! Cluey talk to me now!! Cluey manages to collect herself for a moment. (Sobbing) It's......it's my baby brother Veil, he's been in a bad accident. He was riding his bike home and someone hit him and he was thrown into a tree. Oh Perfect, It's bad it's really bad, Oh please come to the hospital, I need you here, I don't know if he's is going to make it, please come quickly. You're my best friend I need you. Perfect quickly shouts into the phone Okay okay, I'm on my way. I'll be there in just a few minutes, just try and come down. Perfect leaps off her bed, she's already dressed, she puts her shoes, and runs out of the door. She gets to the hospital, in record time, and enters the emergency room. Cluey, her family, and friends are all there sobbing and consoling one another over the young Theirkind boy's condition. Cluey sees Perfect entering the room, with a nurse fast on her trail, saying miss miss you can't go in there, only immediate family is allowed. Cluey signals to the nurse that it's okay. Perfect and Cluey embrace in a strong sister hug. Cluey takes Perfect over to the bedside where the lifeless boy is lying. The small boy has lacerations all over his body, a large badge on his head, which encases a large wound, that is still bleeding, which is right now is the biggest threat to his life. The doctor is in the room checking the boy's vital signs and reading his chart. He takes a moment and speaks to the family he says, that everything that can be done for the boy is being done, but unfortunately the boy's condition does not look good at this time, the deepest lacerations are on his head, we are trying to control the bleeding, if we cannot completely control the bleeding over the next 3 hours he could bleed to death. And if he makes it through the night he will only have a 15% chance of survival, at this point, it will take of some kind of miracle, for him if he survives his injuries at all. Perfect, Cluey, Sin, family members, and the doctor are all standing at the boy's bedside. Perfect looks at the wails of tears in her friend's eye and how upset and terrified she looks. She watches her friend's parents embrace each other in their sadness and pain. Perfect thinks to herself, I feel so helpless, if I only knew what to do, if there was only something I could do. She stares into space for a moment and repeats to herself what the doctor said, it would take some kind of miracle to help him, a miracle to heal him, a miracle healing. It's late night, Perfect is still in the room seated at the bedside of the young child. The lights in the hospital halls are deemed visiting hours are long pasted. Family and friends are still there. She gets up and goes out into the waiting room, where she sees all the family members and friends are asleep. She slips out one of the hospital through a janitor's door leaving it slightly open. She shows up at Marley's house unannounced knocking on her door. Marley is asleep, but she hears the knocking on the door, she sits up in her bed, turns on the lamp on her night stand, and looks at the clock that reads 01:05 am. Not knowing who it is, she gets up from her bed and goes to the door. She peers out of the peep hole, to see Perfect, standing at her door. Marley opens the door Perfect stares at her and she ask if she can come in. Marley says; yes. Once inside Marley asked; Perfect what's wrong? Why are you here at this hour? Perfect says; (rubbing her hands) I'm sorry about the hour, but I had to come over here. There's been an accident, my friend's little brother is hurt bad, the doctor doesn't think he is going to survive the night, he's bleeding badly, they said if they can't completely control the bleeding he might not survive the night. Marley gasped, oh no Ms. Perfect I'm so sorry. The doctor said it would take a miracle, if he pulls through the next few hours. Marley replies; I'm truly sorry to hear about the young boy, so what brings you here? I was thinking about everything you told me about Mercy and how he healed you, and Nervius, and myself. Marley replies; Ms. Perfect I know what you're thinking, and I know you want to help your friend's little brother, but don't you think that would be taking an awful risk, for the child, as well as yourself. Perfect responds; (Holding her hands in the air) I don't want to hear the negatives, I already know, I thought about all of that on the way over here, I don't care about me, I just can't stand by and do nothing. I have to do something, and besides everyone was asleep when I left, and I can get in and get out, before anyone knows anything. She looks at Marley with tears in her eye and says; Marley, I have to try this no matter what the risk. Now no more talking about it. Come and help me get Mercy ready. Marley backs off and doesn't say another word. She leads Perfect go down the hall to the bedroom where the babies are sleeping, she enters the bedroom where Mercy is asleep, and proceeds to get him dressed, placing blankets over him and they leave for the hospital. She enters the same way she left through the janitor's back door. She's upstairs, she looks around to make sure that everyone is still fast asleep. She goes into the young boy's room. She unwraps the blankets and places Mercy on the boy's head near the blood stains gauge bandage. Nothing happens at first and then Mercy tiny body illuminates, where the blood stains bandages were once wet, they starts to dry up and turn dark. As Mercy glows the gauge are drying out. From deeply within the boys head, the flesh begins to knit back together the gaping wound now starts to close, as the layers of skin starts to rejoin on the boy's head, Perfect lifts a corner of the bandage to witness the progress. The wound is now closing as the skin has completely knitted back together and a huge scab beings to form, the crusting of the scab first soft begins to slowly harden until it turns into a hard scab. Soon the large hard scab has completely replaced the gaping wound, then scab begins to shrink in size and falls off. Under the scab is a huge shinny discolored scar that takes its place and then the scar starts to fade in stages as of shadows of its self, getting more invisible and smaller until it has camouflaged into the natural color of the boy's complexion. And all the other lacerations are healed about the young boy's body. Perfect replaces the blood soaked gauge, smiles, gives the boy a kiss, looks around, and picks up her miracle baby gives him a gentle kiss. She carefully wraps him back in the blankets, and quietly leaves the hospital through her secret escape route. She returns Mercy safely back to Marley's house. Marley opens the door and her and Perfect stare at each other, they don't immediately exchange words. She walks in Marley ask, how did it go? Perfect replies; it went very well, the child is healed. I don't think anyone saw me, everyone was still asleep. Marley replies; well I am glad that you could help the child. But Ms. Perfect you do know that, come morning there will be many probing questions and suspicions as to how the child became healed overnight. Marley expressed to her; that going forward we must

be very careful. Perfect nodded her head that she under-
stood. Perfect gave Mercy a sweet kiss and handed him over to
Marley to put to back to bed. Marley put Mercy down and
returned to the living room where Perfect was seated. Well
Mercy is all tucked in, this has been an absolutely draining
night for me and I'm sure for you too. I was so worried for the
both of you. Perfect said; I'm sorry for waking you up and
worrying you. But I felt that something had to be done, to
help my friend. And maybe with this, I could do something
right in my life, for the first time in a long time. Just then
they heard talking coming from another room. Perfect
asked; who is that? Marley explained that she was a distant
cousin and older lady. She was now taking care of. She was
quite expressive but harmless. And that she would be staying
with her. Lots of talking coming from Ms. Likey's room. She
repeats everything she thinks about. Ms. Likey speaking;
IT'S GOD'S WILL! IT'S GOD'S WILL! IT'S GOD'S
WILL! WATCH THE DEVIL! WATCH THE DEVIL!
WATCH THE DEVIL! Marley sees Perfect out. Perfect returned home totally exhausted but, feeling good about the
night's accomplishments. She awaken to a breaking news report on television, the topic A MIRACULOUS RECOVERY.
A breaking news conference is at the hospital, the physician
that was attending the badly injured boy, was also the hospital
Chief of staff. He was at the podium to make his statement.
Also there was the WBI (Willowiest Bureau of Investigates) at
the podium about to make a statement. They were called in
due to the unexplainable, miraculous recovery of the young
boy, overnight. It shocked the staff found the boy fully

recovered and all injuries healed. On behave of the staff here at Willoweist General we are in awe of the unexplainable recovery of the boy, and we are still puzzled by the recovery that took place just within the last 7 hours, never seen anything like it, nothing short of a miracle. But nevertheless we are happy that his condition has drastically improved, but we will keep him here and continue to monitor his condition until we feel it will be okay for him to return home with his family. We would like to thank you all for all of your well wishes and kindness. Thank you. The next speaker was a member of the WBI he takes the podium; I will be brief but direct, as a representative of the WBI we feel that there are unexplainable mysterious circumstances, surrounding the miraculous recovery of this boy's condition, and we will be launching a full and complete investigation. We believe there may have been the possibility of witchcraft that may have played a part in this overnight phenomenon and as we all know witchcraft is forbidden. There will be a full investigate and if we find evidence of any unlawful activities that took place as it relates to this case, we will find those perpetrators responsible for this and they will be brought to justice. So for we have secured one lead. The WBI Agent held up a tiny blue blanket. We will be investigating where this blanket came from it had no reason for being in the boy's room. Except perhaps it was dropped by the suspect in question. Perfect gasped; Oh no! The WBI Agent continues. We believe this evidence was left at the scene and we will be conducting test on this blanket to find out where it came from, what part of the island it was purchased, and who or to whom it may belong too. Perfect sit

in her bed with her hand over her mouth frozen. Oh my
goodness how could I have been so careless? I must have
dropped it as I was leaving the room. About that time Perfects
phone rings its Marley she's seen the new bulletin. Perfect
picks up the phone. Hello hi Perfect it's me Marley. Perfect
leaps ahead of the conversation. Hey I know it looks scary, but
we must keep our cool they want link the blanket to us, don't
worry everything is going to be all right. Marley speaks up;
Ms. Perfect I have those blankets all over my house. I think
it's time to move the babies. Perfect; Marley don't panic.
Marley; I'm not panicking just concerned and I know that
you aren't concerned about this but I hear that the revolution
has started, I see the protest on the news every day and it's
getting worse, I think it's time to think about moving the
babies to a safer place. Perfect pipes up; what do you mean a
safer place? I heard that some of the defectors are considering a neighboring island, where there are no rules and laws
to prevent us from living as we want to live united together as
one group. Perfect replies; Marley I don't know about all that
and how will I see by baby. Marley replies; we all can go. Ms.
Perfect just think about it Mercy and the others will be safer
there, they want be judge for who they are. Perfect replies;
Marley; I have to think about all of this, my child and his
safety. And what about my parents, I just don't want to leave
them. Perfect says; if this is real, I have a lot to think about.
Marley says; well if nothing else listen closely among the
young One eyes Theirkinds, they are the ones to pay attention too. Because here on the island, they are upset with the
system and laws in place there's talk of the council's planning

a retaliation against them. Perfect replies; well we will keep our eyes on the situation and see where it goes. But for now I'm not moving my baby. Look I have to go. I'm late for work. I'll talk to you soon. They hang up.

7

Sin Calls Perfect

Sin: (Perfect gets a call from Sin) Hi Perfect Perfect replies; hi what's up? Sin replies; oh not much. Hey I need to talk to you about something Perfect responses; what is it? Sin replies: I really don't want to get into it over the phone with you. How about I come by your place today? Perfect responds; Look Sin I'm really tired how about us getting together tomorrow sometimes? Sin laughs; this can't wait. Perfect sighs; can you just tell me what this is about right here right now? Sin: Okay have it your way. You remember the other night when we all were at the hospital, when we thought Cluey's little brother wasn't going to make it? Prefect; yes I do. Sin; (lowering her voice) well I saw you

Perfect nervously says; what do you mean? You saw me what? We all was there. Sin; (Whispering) my dumb one I saw you later, much later, in the hospital. I saw you when you left, I saw when you returned, I saw what you had, I saw what you did, and I saw you when you left again. I........saw.....you. Must I go on? (Perfect takes a hard swallow because she knows now perfectly well what I saw you meant but she still tries to play it off as if it was nothing) Perfect; okay so what you saw me......And? Sin says; I think you know now we need to talk. I'm standing outside your door. If you're home you need to let me in? Perfect gets up from her couch and goes to her front door, and sure enough there stands Sin on her door step. Blazing red in all of her glory. Perfect opens the door to Sin. She walks in, the two young women look at each other, and then they take a seat at Perfect's kitchen table. Sin begins; I'm usually quite direct. I am known not to mix my words. I'm Sin baby I seldom sleep. As I said I saw you the other night. I saw you go into that boy's room with something, and I saw you leave. And the next morning he's fine. I'm here to find out what it was. I want to know what it was in those blankets. Don't play with me. What did you used to heal that boy? We all knew that boy was finished. So you might as well come clean with me. Something that can heal like that I want in on it. And I wanna know what it is now. Sin sits back on her chair, you know typically, nothing impresses me. But that impressed me. Little miss pretty Perfect. Got a big ole nasty secret. Sin extends her arms toward Perfect to start talking. Perfect looks petrified her secret is out, she clears her throat; it's a long story. Sin snaps looking at her watch:

Good I've only got the rest of my life. Let's hear it. Perfect starts; something happened to me some months ago. Sin: And what was that? Perfect says; (nervously) I AH some months back I....... ah.......had had a baby. Sin replies; oh a baby.........cute....... keep going. Perfect nervously explaining; he was born with Two Eyes, he can fly, and he has a gift to heal. Sin replies; against the law, crazy, and unbelievable. Wow even more impressive. So now let me understand you. Some months ago, you secretly had a baby which you kept secret away from me, your parents, and your best friend Cluey. This baby that you had can heal injuries, he has two eyes, and he can fly. Now you do know, this is about the craziest crap, I have ever heard of in my entire life? If I had not witnessed seeing you go into that room with the bundle in the blankets and the fact that it is you Perfect sitting here telling me this story? I would not have believed anything that you just told me. So that explains why we saw you that day in town with a baby stroller. Very interesting Per... Now let's see how we can take this valuable information and put it to good use. And idea pops into Sin's head. I know I have a plan how we can make a ton of money. An all cure miracle business. We can start a miracle cure business. Perfect snaps at her; No we want! You're not using my baby like that. Sin replies; Perfect Perfect don't be stupid now, either you help me with this business, or I'll go straight to the freakin authorities, and I'll have you and your freak baby brat thrown in jail, for practicing witchcraft Perfect shouts; you wouldn't! Sin snaps; Girl my name is Sin try me. Yes the hell I would. After all, I'm here by invitation only, you opened the door I walked in.

Perfect responses; you wouldn't go the authorities you're supposed to be my friend. Sin replies; Right now I'd like to think of us as business partners. I don't have any friends. Perfect you really don't know me all that well. Let me tell you something's about my history, I'm the product of a brutal rape, and my grandfather was also my father. My mother said she named me Sin as a monument of disgrace to her father. Although they are no longer physically here, the essence of them lives on forever inside of me. I was born because of sin, while being born into sin. And I live for the sake of sin. I proudly live up to my name each and every day I can. Control, power, jealousy, envy, temptation, death, and destruction. My social circles are limitless, my associates are many, if you allow me to control one part of you, I can control all of you. My purpose is not to cure I could care less if they lived or died, I'm just here to collect the money. Perfect says; go to hell Sin. Sin replies; I have two condo's and a beach house there. You're not doing it, well get ready to smile pretty for the cameras. Perfect: But Sin money isn't everything. Sin snaps; you spoiled rich brat it is to me. Sin pauses for a moment then she begins; Perfect we only knew each other in college, so you really don't know anything about me. I didn't come up with money the way you did. Although my parents and I were One Eyes they had nothing. I had to sleep my way through college and do you know how many disgusting fat baldheaded married Deans I had to sleep with so I could get my college tuition paid in full. Perfect's mouth drops open Sin: That's right I love money. Don't judge me. With money you have control and with control you have power and with power you can conquer anything. Look you invited me into your life when you opened your door to me. Let's keep this business like and get to it. Sin stands up. I have to run now. Get head in the game. I will be calling you once I secure some clients. Let's put our petty difference aside and let's make some money here. Sin leaves Perfect's house. Perfect is sitting there not knowing what she would do next so she calls Marley. Hi Marley can I come by I need to see you. Marley says sure and Perfect is sitting at her breakfast table in 20 minutes. Perfect explains to Marley the dilemma she's found herself in Marley is terrified for her. Marley scolds her. Ms. Perfect I warned you to be careful. Perfect states; I know you did, my secret is out now, but what other choice do I have. Marley replies; but the outcome is never good when making a deal with a devil. Perfect replied; I know I thought she was my friend. But Marley I only told her about Mercy. I promise you I will never tell her about the others. Marley explains hopefully the revolution will be a saving grace. Perfect asked what revolution. Marley continue to explain, a revolution to change the laws here on Willowiest. So that everyone on the island will be treated equally. Perfect says and how do you know that? Marley says oh I hear things. But that will make a great difference for all of us. If the Counsels of Willowiest doesn't put a stop to it. But Yahweh will make a way. Perfect looks at her and says oh here you go with that higher power stuff again. Marley says is it better to hope for what can be as to holding on to something where there is no hope. Perfect looks at Marley and smiles. Hey Marley thank you for letting me come over and vent. Seems to me you are the only person

I can talk to anymore. I'm too afraid to turn to anyone about this. Thank you for listening. Marley smiled at her and held out her arms they embrace in a hug and Perfect goes home. Once at home she turns on the television to get the news. She watches a disturbance of some kind downtown in front of the Councils of Willowiest offices. Its young One eyed Theirkinds protesting, carrying signs, and shouting let our friends go! Lock up the right ones. If they did the crime let them do the time! The police was standing between the protestors and the front doors of the Councilman of Willowiest offices. They were astounded they had never witnessed anything like this before. The police were locked arm in arm but did not arrest them. The chief said to let them blow off their steam and they would soon go home. But they did not go home they protested all night. Meanwhile Sin's business venture had commenced.

8

Healing Business

As promised Sin calls Perfect about their business venture. Hello there Perfect we've got our first appointment scheduled for tonight. Have that brat. I mean the child ready to go. I'm sending you the assignments via text. Perfect is very quiet on the other end of the phone. Sin snaps; Are we clear on this? Do you understand? Perfect replies; yes we are clear I understand. Sin replies; Oh Per don't sound so drab. We're making money. I love money. And just so there's no misunderstandings, I will be there and you'd better show up or else and follow my instructions to the letter Perfect replies; I will. Shortly after they hang up.

Perfect receives a text from Sin with the first patient with the nursing home facilities she has to visit. Her first stop was Forget me not retirement home. Perfect and Marley make a plan to change the babies up that way the babies are not burned out and Sin would never know the difference. At the first appointment, Perfect takes Favor with her. Sin is there waiting for them. Sin says; you are on time very good. Now let's get this show on the road. Sin explains this is Ms. Dowdy, this old geezer, has a heart problem, and her family wants it fixed. So get the kid and let's get to it. Perfect brings Favor over to the patient, unwraps him from his blankets and places the baby on the chest of the woman. At first nothing happens, then the warm loving glow of Favor's little light increased, the tones of the hospital monitors start to change, from erratic warning signals, unstable infrequent heart beats, to a more consistent rhythm. ___^*^____>>__@ ___^___>>__@___*#^^$^____ As the heart valves outputs and inputs becomes more smooth and streamline the rise and fall of her chest becomes more at ease and less labored. The heart rate transforms from a diseased faint irregular beat into a strong stable healthy heart rate. The heart is healed __^_^_^_^_^_^_^_^_. The patient is now resting comfortable and sleeping peacefully. Perfect removes Favor from the patient's chest wraps the baby up and they leave. Back at Marley's house Perfect is distraught at how she could find herself in such a fix. I don't even understand their powers or how strong they are. Marley says; well the good thing is, Sin can't tell the babies apart they all are about the same age.

We will change them out for the appointments, keep them dressed all the same, she will never know. But you will at least be meeting her demands and none of the babies will get burned out.

Sin waited until the money cleared the bank before she takes the next appointment. Once the money is clear. She instructs Perfect to come back to the same nursing home, and on to the next client. Meanwhile, Perfect has refused to take a dime from Sin's greedy extortion money from the elderly Theirkinds. This time Perfect takes Mercy on the appointment she takes him from his crib and enters the room. Sin goes in with them Sin explains Mr. Timberlock's condition; this old fart has smoked like a chimney for 35 years. He ran his own cold mining company and was inside the mines everyday so needless to say his lungs are shot he needs some detox magic. There was a mine collapsed some months back and he was lucky they found him and pulled him out he's been unconscious ever since. So let's get started. Sin pulls the breathing ventilator out of his mouth, he starts gasping for breath. Perfect places Mercy on the chest of the patient, as with Mercy it started slowly, as the child begins to glow and the process begins with Mr. Timberlock. He moves his head back and forth, he's coughing up dry heaves, and then something comes out of his mouth that appears to be black dust, it starts to shoot out of his mouth. Then a black thick substance like tar starts to ooze from his mouth. Perfect is disgusted but looks on in disbelief. They cringe at the look of all the tar coming out of him. His struggle to breathe becomes a lot less, it was so much gunk that expelled through his mouth from his chest, and it was all over the bed and floor. Mercy sit sweetly and quite, is enjoying the ride of the rise and fall of his chest; soon he was breathing comfortable and was breathing completely on his own. He went from breathing 70% on the machine 30% on his own, his breathing was now100% on his own. The patient was healed. Perfect packs up the miracle baby and they leave. The next week rolls around and this time she takes Grace with her. Sin and Perfect park the baby stroller in the hall and she picks up Grace and they go into the room. Sin explains Mr. Matthias had an accident he has a large wound that is not healing on his leg, he's been here for weeks. Sin explains; this loser's wife left him for another Theirkind and he just started drinking and ran his car off an embankment. He was admitted here and has been clinging to life. The money has cleared so let's go to work. Mr. Matthias has a chronic case brain damage. He has been none responsive for a couple of years. In a vegetation stage, and deteriorating fast. Perfect looks at Sin and says I know the routine. She places Grace on Mr. Matthias head and thus the process began. Little Grace sat quietly and started to glow. Mrs. Matthis begins to moan. She had not spoken a word in months, she starts talking, calling for her children, family members, and husband. Her brain functions were normal all cells are renewed. Sin turns up her pain drip and she goes back off to sleep. Sin says; Okay let's get out of here once outside she says, girl this kid is amazing at what he does. Our next target is the hospital I'll text you with some more clients next week. I know you're familiar with that aren't you Perfect? Perfect rolls her eye and leaves. Similar appointments would go on until Sin had collected well over 50 million dollars. Miracle cures went on for months. Old Theirkinds that was thought, at one time, a lost cause were up, and out enjoying life with their loved ones again.

9

Cluey and Nervius at the Lunch counter

Cluey is out getting her nails done she makes a stop at this small café for a bite to eat. The hostess seats her at a table and assure her that a waiter will be right with her. The waiter soon arrives greets her a good afternoon and quickly hands her a menu. There was something familiar about the waiter's voice, but she continues looking at the menu, and never looks up. She orders a spritzer, the waiter quickly leaves to place her drink order. He's back with her drink. Then explains that he will give her time to decide on her meal and he would be back. The voice strikes her psyche again and her curiosity peaks so she looks up. The waiter has a menu up to his face, as though he is trying to hide himself.

She's starring at him and she says; hey you sound familiar. Do I know you? He becomes very uneasy and replies; no I don't think so madam. She asks him. Please can you take that menu away from your face? I'd like to see the face of the person that is serving me my meal. He slowly moves the menu to one side, showing only half of his face. She continues to stare at him. Suddenly she says Nervius is that you? The waiter becomes very nervous and responses I don't know what you mean. Nervius that is you? He responded; no it's not. She snaps back at him fool that it is you. Nervius slowly removes the menu with a frantic smile on his face. He responds; yeah it's me. She looks at him in disbelief. She grabs him by the neck tie causing him to bend down to where she is sitting. She says; fool do you know that you've got two eyes now. OMG what's up with that? Nervius takes a hard swallow and says, well it's kind of a long story. Cluey looks down at her cell phone and says I've got time. What…. In….. The…. hell….. Happened….. To….. You? When in the hell did you become a Two Eyes? Nervius takes another hard swallow; well you can start by asking your crazy friend Perfect, she did this to me. She put witchcraft on me and turned me into a Two Eyes. Cluey is sitting there with her mouth wide open. OMG you are kidding me no freakin way…. You sure it didn't come from smoking that stuff? Nervius No No I've been smoking for years and this ain't never happened. Nervius continues. Yeah she got me to go to this house in the valley and there was this baby and it was possessed with witchcraft and I touched it and now I'm….. I'm a Two Eyes. Cluey sits back in her chair OH SNAP OMG SHUT THE FRONT DOOR…..DUDE….

WORD!...... now Perfect is my girl, I don't believe this for a moment. Now Nervius you know you bout a lying ass too. Nervius said I swear to you, it's the truth it happened just like I told you. She's crazy as hell with this demon baby. Yeah you go talk to her ass that's what you do because she's ruined by life. I gotta figure out what my next move is Nervius's boss knobs for him to get back to work. Cluey finishes her meal thinking to herself, a witchcraft baby turned Nervius into a Two eyes? OMG Oh hell nall I'm calling Perfect. She gives Perfect a call. Perfect answers her call. Hello. Hey Perfect this is Cluey where are you? On my way home good I need to come by and see you for a minute do you mind? Perfect says; No what's up? Cluey says, nothing really I just need to talk to you. Perfect says okay that's cool I'll be there. Cluey arrives at Perfects house they set in the living room. Cluey starts; Now Perfect I'm about to tell you something that's gonna blow your mind. Perfect sits forward with anticipation. I just saw somebody we know. Perfect says; who? I just saw Nervius. Perfect takes a hard swallow; oh you did? Yeah and he's changed. Did you know this Mo fo got two eyes now. Perfect takes another hard swallow he does? Yeah and guess what else? Not only did I see him I talked to him and he said it was your fault he looks like that and how you put some witchcraft baby on him and it did a number on his ass. He got jacked. Perfect reposition herself on the couch she starts with her explanation. Look I want lie to you, you are my best friend. There is a lot going on, but I can't say anything right now, I promise when things are better I will tell you everything. Can you trust that? Cluey says sure Per. I mean it's just that Nervius

was saying Perfect cuts her off; he was saying nothing because he doesn't know anything. I just have not been able to
tell you. Cluey says; well whatever it is I trust you and I love
you and be strong. Perfect walks her to the door they hug
once more and then she leaves. Cluey has to pass by the offices of the Councilman of Willowiest to get home, when she
runs into some protestors out on the street with their signs,
stating change these unjust laws now, and free our friends.
Their shouting "No justice No peace. She calls Perfect. Hey
Per turn on your television these protestors are really getting serious. Perfect says I see that. Wow and you know they
are out here every day sometimes all night. Cluey says wow
this is getting so serious. They are really angry about these
laws. Perfect replies I know and if I would think it could help
my situation I would be out there with them. The police just
normally let them have their say and let it die down by itself.
Cluey replied yeah they do. They'll get tired and it will all
blow over and things will get back to normal. But girl I have
to get some rest so I will let you go so you can get home safe. I
will talk too you later. Be careful out there. Cluey said I will.
They hang up. But the protesters did not go away there were
more and more that would show up each day, they were some
that was driven. Until the big party bash.

10

The Great Divide

The annual upscale social event of the year, was given each year at one of the private mansions on the island up in the hills. All the A listers would be there for this swank affair. Limousines arriving to drop their distinguish guest. There was music playing throughout the mansion. Waiters and waitresses all dressed in their formal black and white entire serving the guest. Exotic Ice sculptures everywhere. There were plenty of activities going on throughout the mansion for everyone. Like gambling tables, card playing, live entertainment, a show was going on in the main dining area. Then there were exclusive social rooms, that was set up by the more progressive younger one eyes, where the laws of the land were ignored, and folks could just go and hang out. One eyes, Two eyes, and Three eyes were all partying together, dancing, socializing, and mingling together. These rooms were downstairs where a beautiful outlet into a lavish pool area was. Where Their kinds, of all kinds were out there swimming, soaking in the saunas. This was a great time for everyone to get to know each other on one social level. The party lasted well into the night. Just when the party was at its peak. Everybody was feeling their drinks many that weren't dancing started dancing and singing. One of the guest a councilmember was outside smoking. He looked around and saw there were far too many cars outside for all the party goers to be in only a few areas of the mansion. So he stopped one of the waiters and asked. I would like to know where all the parties are going on throughout the mansion. The waiter gave the councilman directions to where all the guest were partying throughout the mansion. The councilman found his way downstairs. He was shocked to find, One eyes, Two eyes, and Three eyes were hanging out, mingling, partying, and socializing. In the corner of the room there was a couple, a One eye and two eyes they were making out. Well he was just appalled at what he saw. This pissed the councilman off. He excused himself from the room. Once out in the hall he called one of his buddies at the police station. He said hey do you know about the party at the mansion tonight? The voice replied yeah some of our officers are working the party as security officers. Well they've got some illegal stuff going on over here and I want you to do a raid on the party and break it up. Really? You want us to raid the party at the mansion, this is the biggest social event of the year. Hey lots of folks really look forward to this every year? The councilman said I don't care they're over here breaking the law and I don't like it. Hey give me about 15 minutes to get out of here then send them in. The voice on the other end says okay you're the boss. The councilman made his way outside and to his car. His house is only a few blocks away, by the time he gets home and showers he could hear the sirens in the distance approaching the neighborhood. Soon the sirens were very loud. They had arrived at the mansion. Paddy wagons were brought to arrest any law breakers. The owner of the mansion asked what is going on here why are you raiding my home. No one has done anything wrong here. The officer responded; so what are all these Two eyes and Three eyes doing here all dressed up? Don't tell me they're the help. This was called in that there were illegal social mingling going on here. And we are here to arrest any law breakers. So the police started going throughout the mansion rounding up all of the Two eyes and Three eyed Theirkind at the mansion they were arrested and thrown in jail. All total was about 185 of them. A lot of the party goers were infuriated having to watch their friends, companions, associates, secret loves, handcuffed and carted away. But they knew they could not say anything for fear of retaliation. After the police were gone. One of the guest received a text message on his phone that one of the party goers a Two eyes was badly beaten on back of one of the paddy wagons and had died. One of the party goers a One eye spoke up as folks were leaving the party. He told them what he just received on his phone. Can't you all see the travesty in this? Folks this is wrong. He was a good man all he wanted to do is have some fun. We should have the right to socialize with whomever we please. We must do something about these laws. They did not deserve to be arrested he did not deserve to die for socializing. We are still here but our Two eyed and Three eyed brethren are in jail. Not because of what they did, but because of who they are. Who will stand with us? About half walked away and half raised their hands. They held what would be the first of many protest at the time square. Unknowingly to those that were so upset by the actions of the police were the same ones the babies had sat on their heads in the fraternity building. And now they were igniting they first revolution on the island. They signed partitions and took their concerns to the council by a strong show of numbers. Trying to get the laws changed that were unfair to their friends. But their grievances and concerns fell on death ears. The council would not budge. So they took their protest and rallies to the streets. Marching first once a day to marching three times a week. To marching and chanting every day. Carrying large signs that read: IT'S TIME FOR SOCIAL FREEDOM! EQUALITY JUSTICE AND SOCIAL INDEPENDENCE! And the chanting and marches were grew larger each day. NO JUSTICE NO PEACE NO JUSTICE NO PEACE NO JUSTICE NO PEACE!!!! FREE OUR BROTHERS!!! One spokesman got up to speak. He said; brothers and sisters the word freedom is a beautiful word. It is an uncontainable word all by itself. But that same word when used in the right way can be a tricky and it can deceive many. We are monitored daily by cameras everywhere we go and everything we do. My question to you is if we are constantly monitored are we truly free. But my brothers and sisters the same concept applies to everything else, we are being contained and controlled by outdated laws that no longer belong in our society. The laws were set in place for the serve the few and control the many. But I say they are there to control us all. It's time for us to take a stand on the behalf of our brethren's the Two eyes and Three eyes for everyone. I know a lot of them and they are good folks. They don't deserve this. Enough is enough. Not only were they wrongfully jailed they had to pay large fines just to be free. This must stop and this must change. When the news of the protest gotten back it infuriated the council. But they were patient with them hoping they would just go away. But they did not go away. Because they were determined to change the laws. So each day a rally would be held in different parts of the island rallying for new members to join their cause. They organized marches, at first peaceful protest, and then the Willowiest police came to one of the protest one day and started pushing the protesters around. The next day they had a sit in on the steps of the council city hall. Many had been arrested for breaking the social laws. One Eyes were secretly dating, befriending, and socializing, Two eyes and Three eyed Theirkinds. They were not only unhappy with the laws of the land, but were up in protest daily of wanting change. And so the great divide begins. These young One Eyed Theirkinds now with untainted minds were dreamers, they thought outside the box, they could care less about money, or preserving a creed. They wanted control over their own lives. They were so angry about the social injustices, they renamed themselves the TOOKIES meaning The Other One Eyed Theirkinds. Their slogan was fair, equal and strong. They planned protest right outside the councilmembers meeting halls, every time the councilmembers would be have a meeting. To disrupt their meetings. A young One eyed Theirkind male was caught dating a Two eyed young woman she was arrested and put in jail for a month. This is one of many arrest that in ignited more protests. Each day in many areas of the city they would protest. NO CHANGE NO PEACE! NO CHANGE NO PEACE! WE WANT OUR SOCIAL FREEDOMS! They would shout. They wanted to worship, believe in whomever or whatever they wanted, be it a higher power, or none at all, and or even false idols if they choose too. Many TOOTKIES and Two Eyes and Three Eyes had many friendships but had to remain secretive, they were falling in love, befriending one another, sharing meals, socializing. And it was strictly forbidden for them to mate and have children. Because the children of what the council called inbreed, were considered to be born insane, cursed, and disfigured. The Supreme Counsels threaten sent a letter to the revolutionaries that if they did not to cease and assist they would take away their status of wealth, if they did not abandon their unheard of behavior and stick to the status quo. But the TOOKIES resentment only grew greater in protests and marches grew larger and with many that became angry and very outspoken. Finally the protest turned violent. They set a building on fire downtown.

As things grew day by day more hostile on the island. Perfect watched all the chaos play out on the news. She knew that it would be only a matter of time until she would have to make a move to protect her baby. The police had begun raiding many homes in retaliation against the protesters, unfairly jailing many two and eyed Theirkinds. But she held out hope that when the time was right, that she would be able to go to her folks and get the help and support from them she so desperately needed.

11

The Revolution

As buildings burn the revolutionaries dominated the news. Street protest, picket signs, the more of the two eyes and three eyes were arrested the larger and uglier the protest became. There were lunch counter sit ins, and the police would come in and remove them from the counters and jail more two and eyes. And every time they were jailed another building would be set afire. The Willowiest Councilmen had to have police escorts to and from work. And a police patrol car in their neighborhoods. Until finally, the Supreme councils of Willowiest had had enough. They held a secret meeting and decided to vote the revolutionaries off the island. One member stood up immediately and shouted this is no more than treason! It's time to put a stop to this! Others joined in shouting we must stop this madness now! This is our land and they must obey our laws or else. Kilgore Perfect's father took the stand saying, now now brethren's, you know it is against the law to kill a One eye. We can't take the life of a Two eyes or Three eyes without inciting more violence. How shall we proceed with this since there are no laws for affluent one eyes. Another member stood and said we have to do something or they will destroy everything on the island. We have to stop them now! So they took a vote. It was unanimous they voted the rebellious One eyes off the island. They waited until the rebellious One eyes were assembled for their evening protest. The police came in and surrounded them, they brought several paddy wagons, and carted them all off to jail. Later that night a sleeping gas was released throughout the jail cells. The police drugged the protesters. Then they carried out and placed them on trucks. The trucks took the sleeping Theirkinds to the shores of Willowiest where they were placed on boats and the boats were pushed out to sea. Lost at Sea

Now what the councilmen had hoped for, that they would drown in the sea, or that they would be lost at sea. They sailed all night long all of them still unconscious. But they did not die. Their boats came to rest upon an uncharted island, as the boat banging against the shore it awakened one of the radicals, as he awakened, he began to wake the others. They sat up in the boat starring at a new uncharted place sparkling in all its glory before them. It was the most beautiful unin-hibited island they had ever seen. Soon as they all awakened and stepped out of the boat. Looking around as far as their eyes could see, was soft light blue sandy beach, miles of it, pink scrubs that seemed to glow and glisten in the distance. A rainbow met them as they peered over the horizon. The palm tree were yellow and in the distance was a water fall as it poured off the mountain side it patterned the colors of the rainbow, which poured into a lavender colored pond crisp and cool. They could hear the cooing of the island birds up high in the trees. It was peaceful and sweet to the ears. White doves flew over the island in formation. They all gathered on the beach shore. They elected Nervius as their new leader. Nervius called them all together and said; my fellow revolutionaries, we are now out cast from Willowiest Island, they no long want us. This is our new land. This land is beautiful and with rich resources. With some work we can make it our paradise. Our new land will be called Promise, and the crowd cheered they all walked around the island admiring the beauty that beheld them. Then they heard a rumbling sound in the distance, they noticed something moving in the brush, they froze in their tracks, it moved through the brush very fast. It was a herd of large cat like beast that came upon them. The large beasts appeared out of the brush. They revolutionaries' became very frightened. Nervius said; don't make any sudden moves, maybe they won't hurt you. So the other Theirkinds did as they were told. The large beast had them surrounded and the beast began to sniff them. They continued to sniff them, walking around the Theirkinds, then they started to lick their legs and hands. Nervius knew in order to keep his position as leader; he had to do something, so he commanded them to just let the beast lick on them. He said; I don't think they're here to harm us. I think they are just curious as to what we are. Another Theirkind said as long as they don't decided that we are food. Nervius said no just let them check us out. They look powerful and strong I think they are tamed. This is something they had never seen before. Nervius with a shaking hand gently started petting one of the large beasts on the head and it bowed before him. He said in a soft voice I think they are friendly. And they all slowly started petting the large beasts on the head and all the beasts started bowing before them. Nervius said; we're safe let's start moving back toward the shore, and we will see if they will follow us, at that moment, another Theirkind in their group said look up he pointed at the hillside of a mountain, there were three more great cat like beasts, standing at the mountain top overlooking the island. And they were all white as snow and magnificent in beauty. One the largest beasts of the herd with a beautiful large white mane and the other slightly smaller beasts with an identical beautiful white mane, they were perceived to be father and son. The other large cat like beast had a golden mane that glowed. They only stood and watched with caution every move the Theirkinds made. They stood as leaders' would stand, motionless and powerful. And then suddenly the largest beast leaped from the mountain side and took flight with his magnificent huge golden wings which were obscured by the clouds surrounding the mountain. Then his son took flight with his magnificent wings soaring and then circling around the mountain and then they were joined by the third beast with its massive wing span. As the clouds moved over the mountain top. They soon vanished into the clouds as quickly as they had appeared. Nervius spoke to the others no that this is not a curse but a new beginning for us. I think they are here to protect the island and everything and everyone on it. Don't be afraid. Be glad that they are on our side. Another Tookie spoke up. How do you know they are here to protect us? Nervius responds; because if they wanted to hurt us they would have already done so. Let continue our work and make this our new home. Meanwhile back home an epidemic of death unleashes itself across the Willowiest Island. Folks are being found dead in their cars, in their yards, at the beauty salons, in the movies. Death is everywhere. Sin's phone starts ringing off the hook from angry customers. Their relatives have died. And they are demanding their money back. She's on the phone saying; hey Sir sir I don't know what happened. I have to consult with my healer. I will I promise I will get back to you. She hangs up the phone. It rings again. She answers hey yes ma'am I will find out what happen and get back to you, yes I know I got paid. She nervously laughs haven't you heard the wages of Sin is death. Yes ma'am I'm sorry I know that's not funny. I promise I will have this straighten out in 24 hours. Thank you. She hangs up. I've got to find Perfect and that brat!

12

Tragic Returns

Three months later the healed Theirkinds were being found dead, everywhere. Perfect gets a call from Sin. Perfect what is going on here? Perfect responds; what do you mean? Our clients they are dying, Perfect yelps; they are? Sin says; Yes! I just got a call from a couple of customers and their love ones have died, my phone has been ringing off the hook, and now they want their money back! Perfect I need to know what in the hell is going on here? I thought that brat was supposed to heal Theirkinds.

Perfect responded slowly; oh my goodness he does? Sin snaps; well he didn't! Perfect responds; I don't know what to tell you. Sin snaps at her; you need to tell me something quick, Perfect replies; I don't know what happened to them. Sin snaps at her again; all I know if you and that freakin brat, don't want to make the 6 o'clock news this evening, you'd better find out why in the hell these old farts died. Get me some answers soon! And she slams the phone down on Perfect. Perfect puts her phone down shaking her head.

She goes into her room and falls across her bed, her head is hurting, she closes her eye then, she's thinking to herself, what am I going to do, I don't know what happened to those folks, what can I do? Suddenly a thought pops into her head. I know I'll call Marley she'll know. She picks up her phone and dials Marley's number. Marley picks up. Hello Ms. Perfect. Perfect responds; hi Marley how are you doing? Marley responds; I'm good, how are you Ms. Perfect? I'm doing okay. Ah Marley, I'd like to ask you about something, Marley replies; and what would that be? Perfect begins; I just got off the phone with Sin a moment ago, well shortly after she hung up on me. She told me that some of the patients we healed died. Marley set silently on the phone for a few moments.

Perfect said; Marley did you hear me? Marley responds; Ah yes Perfect I did. Perfect says; Marley what do you think is going on? Marley says; Perfect I'm not sure. But the children's powers are nothing to play with. If used for the wrong purpose can really back fire on you. And you can get into a mess if you really don't know how they work. Perfect says; I can see that now. I gotta find out what happened soon or Sin is threating to go to the news and expose us. Marley I need your help.

Marley replies; I will do my best to help you. But first of all you need to understand that, that girl was never a friend, secondly she's evil. Perfect listen to me good, when you allow Sin to control any part of your life it will take over and control all of your life. I know you're not looking for a lecture and you're in a bad spot. So I will try to help you as much as I can. I need you to bring me all the information you can on those patients, come to the house this afternoon, and I'll do what I can to find out what went wrong. They hang up. Its late afternoon.

Perfect is at Marley's they sat in the living room. Perfect gives her all the information on the patients and Marley goes over the information then, excuses herself to her meditation room.

She returns in about 15 minutes and she takes a seat next to Perfect on the couch. Marley begins; Ms. Perfect this first patient here, Ms. Dowdy, had a heart problem. She lived a very recluse, bitter an uneventful life. She lacked compassion for anything or anyone. The measure of her life was sustained through grace which was shown in her possessions. The length of her life was sustained through favor. But her heart was only used for despite, hatred, and regrets. The total of her life's rigidity set in. Her heart had harden beyond repair. You choose to heal her with Favor. As I explained she had that. What her soul needed and what she died from was a lack of Mercy. Marley puts down Ms. Dowdy's file and moves on to the next patient. Mr. Timberlock she opens his file. This patient was apparently a hard worker, he owned a mine shaft, and was often down in the mine, working a long side his employee. He was so controlling, he very seldom delegated anything to his workers. He often checked behind all of his employees and when he did not agree with the way they did something he did it over to his liking. His lungs contained more coal than his workers. There was a mine collapse and he was trapped inside for days. It was by grace that allowed him to own the mine. It was by mercy that they found him in time. You healed him with mercy. What his soul lacked and his lungs needed was Favor. Perfect hung her head in shame. Marley gently patted her hand to comfort her saying. Ms. Perfect it okay you couldn't have known this. Basically he work himself to death. Next was Mr. Matthias. His job was constant stress. His brain was overloaded until the cells started shutting down. He was a tax collector. On his orders families were thrown out of their homes or jailed until they paid up. He never bent the rules and never apologized for anything. Being well taken care of by his family was his grace. The fact that no one killed him was his favor. You healed him with favor. What his soul needed and he never gave anyone else was mercy. And what about Cluey's little brother? He's still alive. Marley says; yes he would be still alive because he was healed out of the act of love not greed. Everyone knows that love is mercy and that is exactly what you healed him with Mercy. Perfect asked; how can I fix this? Marley shook her head no and said; it is nothing that you can do. Ms. Perfect please listen to me. As we live life everything in the spirit comes through in seasons, for reasons, with lessons, that are blessings. The cycle of these folk's lives have adjusted accordingly. All you did was borrowed time that was not yours to give and they had time that was not theirs to have. Mercy, Favor, and Grace healed them only for the gain of money. Sin's pay was correct? Perfect asked; it was? Marley continued; Yes death. It's finished. I would not respond to Sin, let it go and walk away because it's over. The focus now has to be on getting the children to a safe and secure place. Please promise me you will think about moving them off of this island soon. Perfect replied; Marley I know, I see the protesters and it's getting worst each day. I'm not sure what's going to happen next. They soon said their goodbyes. Perfect heads for home. Perfect is at home and she's watching the protesters on television and the retaliations from the council. She decides to go to her parents for help with the baby.

13

Perfect's confession

Perfect went to see her parents, they all are seated in the living room, she's very nervous. Perfect begins; mom dad I needed to see you today, because I have something I need to tell you that you don't know about me. Perfect's father Kilgore leans in; honey you sound so serious over the phone, come on nothing can be that bad, that is why we are here for you. Perfect takes a deep breath and begins again; thank you dad right now that's exactly what I need. Mom and dad some months ago I..........I............I had a baby. Each eye of her parent's grew wide, it's a little boy his name is Mercy, and he is 6 months old. Perfect's mother Patsy perks up my good Perfect are you serious? We have a grandchild. How could you keep something like this from us? Her father pipes in; Perfect honey you got yourself in trouble and didn't come to us? Perfect closes her eye and holds her hands up, signaling for her to wait. Mom dad please let me finish. He...Ah......he......was.......Ah.............he was born a Two Eyes......Perfect's mom and dad facial expression dramatically changed her mother's smiles left the room. Perfect nervously says; let me finish, he is a very special baby. Her father asked in what way? Perfect starts again; well he glows, he can fly, and he can heal sickness. Her parents sit straight up in their seats starring at Perfect for several seconds. Patsy pipes up; Perfect how could you do such a thing to us! Perfect response; mom just a moment ago you were happy to have a grandchild and now in thirty seconds, all that has changed? Patsy speak up again; do you believe what you just told us? What do you expect us to do here? Perfect this is just insane. Perfect snaps: mom it is not insane, this has been my life for the last 6 months, I didn't want to tell you guys for this very reason, you would not understand. You always told me that I could come to you all, no matter what the problem was, and now I get all this push back from you. Kilgore sits unusually quite then he decides to speak. Ah sweetheart, where is this child? Perfect snaps; at this point why does that matter? Why do you want to know that? And dad you haven't said anything. Her father starts; well sweetheart this is all a bit shocking for us wouldn't you agree. You walk in here, sit us down, and then you unleash this outlandish story on us, and just expect us to except it all in one breathe. I mean you gotta give us a moment to swallow this as well. Perfect says; I'm trying too, I came here not only to be honest with you guys, about my life. I'm looking for your support in this, so I need to know if you will accept my baby or not? I need you guys. Kilgore starts; Sweetheart, you know I have always been straight with you right? Perfect nodded her head yes. So I have to deal straight with you now. Perfect a Two Eyes in breaded child, and not to mention that it's against the law. Honey for goodness sake, I am on the council, I help make those laws to protect our kind. So that this very thing would not happen. How would it look if I'm seated on the council, making laws that forbid this very thing, and my daughter is parading around town with a Two eyed baby, that is clearly a product inbreeding? And you expect me to call it my grandchild? Honey you have to be kidding yourself, Perfect's mom chimes in; Perfect the child would never be accepted. These children have been known to be freaks of nature, possessed, with demons. Tears are screaming from Perfect's face she is sobbing. She's thinking to herself Marley was right. She burst out in tears yelling, you guys said that I could come to you with anything and now you're turning your backs on me! Perfect's father speaks up honey why are you even considering keeping this child? This situation can only bring you shame and despair. Perfect shouts at her father; no dad this could only bring you and mom shame and despair. She stands up from the couch with tears flowing. I love my baby, I don't care if he has two eyes or not, and I didn't do what you thought I did! I didn't start out sleeping with a two eyes. He wasn't a two eyes when I slept with him. Perfect's dad snaps up; Perfect do you hear yourself. Honey how do you expect us to take you serious? Your story is getting crazier by the moment dear. Perfect what is going on with you? You use to be so sure of yourself and now honey you just sound confused. Where is the child? And who is keeping it? Perfect continues to sob, then she collects herself and says. I see there is no help here for me. And why do you keep asking me that? Why do you wanna know where my child is? It's obvious, that you don't want anything to do with him. And you better not even think about hurting my child. It's obvious, you two will never love him or accept him as I have. Just forget it mom and dad it's clear to me now, you don't understand and you don't want to understand. I'm out. Perfect grabs her purse and heads for the door. She looks back and says; and by the way I didn't only come here to be honest about my life with you all. I also came to tell you that it is a revolution going on this island and that you two had better consider leaving here, whether you like it or not, Willowiest is on the brink of change. She walks outside, her father immediately walks out behind her. Perfect wait I want to know who's caring for the child. Perfect stops in her tracks, turns in a tearful voice, she says; he's being care for by someone that loves him as much as I do, so don't worry about me or my child. She walks away. He watches her until she was out of sight. He has his cell phone in his hand he makes a call. A voice answers on the other end. Hey did you find anything yet. The voice on the other in says no nothing boss. If they're here on this island, they must be hiding under a rock. Perfect's father Kilgore snaps at the voice on the other end. Then turn every freak rock over on this island until you find those brats. As a member of the council, do you understand the position this puts me in! My family, my career everything is at stake as long as those brats are alive. I am not letting a couple of low class worthless whores jeopardize everything I've worked hard for. I'm doing everything possible to locate them. Some things take time. I don't have time! Just do the damn job. Kilgore takes a deep breath. Look I might be onto something, I need to have my daughter followed for about a three days. I need to know where she's going, who she's visiting, who's coming and going from her house. The voice on the other end laughs wow man that's cold your own daughter. Kilgore snaps shut up you fool. I wouldn't have to do this if you had done your damn job already. So just shut up just do as I say. She just left my house get someone on her now. The voice on the other end says; sure thing boss right away. They hang up. Perfect calls Marley she is crying Marley does not pick up. So her leaves her a message. Look Marley you were right. My parents they don't understand my situation. They will would never accept Mercy. Hey I think we need to make our move tonight. I have to make some stops but I will call you later on and come by tonight. Perfects first stop was to withdraw all of her inheritance before her folks would cut her off. And then she stopped at the cleaners and picked up her dry cleaning. She called Marley back and she answered. Hi Marley you were right. Marley replies; about what honey. Perfect crying; my parents I went to them and they turned me down flat. I will be glad when we get off of this island. I'll see you in a minute. Little does Perfect know that she was being followed? Moments later Perfect pulls up at Marley's house. Marley opens the door, Perfect comes in. Marley said just a moment, let me get the paper from the driveway. Marley goes outside to get the paper she notices a car parked down from her driveway, with a person sitting behind the wheel. She notices his licenses plate it has the letters WC 45451. Those plates are only issued to members of the council. She picks up her paper, pretending not to see the suspicious car, and casually walks back inside shuts the door signaling to Perfect with her hands that there was someone outside. Perfect says; Marley what's going on? Marley points out of her window; Look Ms. Perfect there's someone watching my house. Perfect asked; How do you know that? I went out to get the paper and the car was just there. And get this it has WC and some numbers on it. Perfect says; Marley are you sure? Marley replies; Yes I am. Ms. Perfect are you sure you wasn't followed over here. Perfect says; who would want to follow me? Ms. Perfect did you just have a conversation with your parents about how your baby? Perfect; Yes I did oh no my father. Honey I don't mean to harp on this but your father is on the council for Willowiest. There's a car parked outside of my house with a Willowiest Councilmember tag need I go on. Perfect; What are we going to do? Hey first of all we are going to calm down and put our thinking caps on. This is what we're going to do. First let's keep watching to see if the car leaves. They wait taking turns watching the car that's parked down a little ways from Marley's house. They are planning their move around midnight. About 10 pm they look out and the car is gone. They go into action packing everything they can in Perfect's car to take to the shore to wait for the boat.

14

The move of the babies

Perfect realize that she did not have enough pampers for the babies so she runs to the store and tells Marley to be prepared to make their move when she returns. Marley tells her to be very careful. And that she would be ready when she returned from the store. Marley waiting with anticipation of Perfects return. Someone rings the door and knocks on the door. Marley comes to the door and peeks through the peep hole. There stands a very tall man with two other men in black suites. She recognizes him, its Perfects father Kilgore. Marley says; she takes a deep breath and opens the door she says; yes may I help you? He says; Hello ma'am. I'm from the council. May I come in?

She says yes you may. This tall stern gentlemen walks in. My name is Kilgore and yours. She answers; my name is Marley. He says; it's very nice to meet you. I won't waste your time, I'll get right to it. I would like to know what dealings you have with my daughter. I've been informed that she comes and goes over here quite a bit. Marley caught off guard but quickly recovers. Ah she comes over to take piano lessons from me. Kilgore responds as he's looking around. Oh piano lessons, he walks over to where the piano is in the living room and strokes his glove across it picking up dust from the cover that's closed over the keys. That's interesting because I could never get her to take them before. Marley nervously replies, she decided to take them on her own. He quickly ask. Do you mind if we look around. Marley repeated his last two words, look around no not at all. He and his goons start looking all around her house. He heads to the kitchen at first looking in the refrigerator and then proceeded down the hall to the bedrooms. He's walking from room to room as he's questioning Marley. If you don't mind me asking, what do you do for a living? Marley answers; Oh a little bit of everything. He opens the door to the first bedroom, which was Marley's bedroom, he walks out and goes to the next bedroom, he opens the door to the next room, he see's baby cribs. He asks; Ms. Marley do you keep children? She replies; why yes I do. He asks; how old are these children? She replies; ah they're a year up to two years old, he asked; where are the children now? She response; their parents picked them up earlier. How many children would you say that you keep every day? Marley says; oh between three are four. He walks into the last bedroom he walks out and closes the door and proceeds back to the living room area. He turns to her and says; look the reason for my visit today, it's been rumored that there may be children living in this area that are victims of inbreeding. And of course you know that is against the law to harbor these children. Marley responds; yes I do. He continues; they must be removed and dealt with accordingly. And Marley knew what dealt with accordingly meant. Put to death. He and his goons walks back toward the front door. He turns to her. We will be checking all new-born children up to six months old in this area to make sure they're not suffering from any birth defects. Here's my card if you see anything like that or if someone brings a child for you to care for in less say less than normal condition would you please give us a call. Thank you for your time. Marley responded; sure absolutely. He put his hat on and thanked her for her cooperation and left. Marley watched the large black vehicle back out of her drive away. Marley immediately ran back the bedrooms opening each door desperately, calling to the babies, little sweethearts where are you? She couldn't find them. She finally open the door to the last bedroom and she is looking all around for them and calling to them, she looks up toward the ceiling because that's where they normally play and she heard giggles and then they appeared to her near the ceiling. She started smiling you little ones, you can now disappear, and I didn't know you were up there the whole time, you had me worried. Perfect is on her way back when she gets a frantic call from Marley. Perfect hi Marley how's it going? Perfect I just got a visitor. Perfect says; a visitor who? Your father was just here. Perfect's mouth dropped open. You are kidding me. Marley said; no he was just here, that means he had you followed, he searched the house and was asking questions. Perfect says; asking you questions about what? About why were you coming over here, the children that I keep, how many children and how old were they. And get this he said it was rumored that it was children staying in the area that were victims of inbreeding and how I knew it was against the law. Perfect yelped; oh my, he's looking for my baby, because he kept asking me who was keeping my child and I wouldn't tell him. Marley replies; Oh Ms. Perfect I'm scared we've to get out of here tonight.

Perfect and Marley's journey to Promise

And so they did, at midnight Perfect, Marley and all three babies, was at the shore waiting on the boat. And sure enough at the stroke of midnight the boat appeared out of the darkness, they boarded the boat along with many others and they sailed away from the shores of Willowiest. The babies were all asleep. Perfect dropped a tear as she thought of leaving her parents behind, but she knew now, she had to think of herself and the safety of her child. They awakened to the morning light and the boatmen docking ashore on Promise. They peered at their horizon and behold it was beautiful, new, clean, and fresh. They could see the progress of cranes, and houses being built, buildings some finished and some not. A guide met them and gave them registration papers showed them to their temporary housing. Perfect and Marley were quite impressed at the well-organized way in which they were taking care of. As they stood in line the babies wake up and they wanted to play. Perfect is reluctant to let the little ones out of their blankets. She looks at Marley and says what should we do? I'm scared to let them out of the blankets. Marley says; well Perfect they said here they will be accepted, there's no better time to find out than now. Let them go. Perfect looks so scared but she unwraps the babies and let them go they start floating and playing with each other. The other Theirkinds gathered around them and they started smiling and pointing at the beautiful babies as they flew around and played. One kinsman asked; oh they are so beautiful are they all yours? Perfect and Marley look at each other and at the same time they said they're ours. Checking in to Promise was in deed a process, there were long Customs lines. They finally got through the long check in process. Perfect had requested that Marley stay with her and the babies. She was granted her request. Once in their new place which was beautiful. The nursery was already set up so they put the babies down for a nap. They unwind with a cup of tea out on their beautiful deck with an ocean view. They reclined in the soft white plush deck chairs. Marley looked at Perfect's face which expressed that something was still on her mine. She asked Ms. Perfect what's going on with you. Perfect replied; I'm still wondering about my parents and if they got out in time. Oh dear hopefully they did and perhaps you'll see them very soon. Marley hesitates a moment and she says Perfect honey I have to share something with you. Perfect looks at Marley giving her her complete attention. She ask what is it Marley. Marley takes a sip of her tea and places it on the table. She starts slow ah you remember when you asked me about the parents of the other babies Favor and Grace. Perfect replies yes. Well the mother of Grace was a two eyed young woman a prostitute, who showed up on my door step one day with Grace in a basket not long before you did with Mercy and she dropped that child off but she said that she did not know when she could return to check on the child because she had been threaten by the father. She said that she was being followed and that she feared for her life. I asked her about the father of the child and she told me that she knew things about the council in Willowiest that she had no business knowing that could destroy them all. Involving young girls Theirkind trafficking and other accusations. I asked her what that had to do with the father of her child. She broke into tears, she said that she was brutally raped by the father and that he was a powerful figure. And no one would ever believe her. She said that she was ordered by the father to destroy the child before it was born. But she said that she couldn't do that. So she brought the baby to me. I'm sorry Ms. Perfect but she also revealed to me who the father was. Perfect asked; who is it? Marley sadly replied; she said it was Kilgore your father, I'm so sorry. Perfect gasped; my father putting her hand up to her mouth with tears started rolling down her face. And Favor's mother is a three eyes that was raped also by him also, and she brought me Favor one week before Grace arrived. Unfortunately, there was a news report not long after that of a young two eyed woman found dead in a field several miles outside of town. And then another report of a young three eyed woman found in a dumpster behind a building downtown. I have not seen or heard from either of them since then. That's why I know it's time to move. Because if he had them followed he's was having you followed too. I knew it was time to leave. Somehow he knows the children are alive and he was looking for them to kill them. Ms. Perfect I'm so sorry for having to tell you this but it was something I could not continue to keep from you any longer. Perfect holding her hand up motioning for Marley to stop speaking about it, while shaking her head from side to side in silence and shock of what she just heard. She manages to speak no I'm okay Grace and Favor are my little brother and sister. Marley walks over to her puts her arm around Perfect's shoulders looks at her and smiles; yes they are sweetheart. Perfect dries her tears and strengthens herself and says well Marley I can't worry about that now, what he has done, he has done. Those were his decisions and not mind. Just then Perfect's phone rings. She picks it up without looking at it. It's Sin. Hi Perfect where are you? Perfect responds; I'm not at home right now. Sin snaps; I know that I'm at your house, hey it's really getting crazy around here, businesses are closing, and I don't know where all the help has gone. You need to come home now. You never got back with me. I still got these crazy people calling me talking about we took their money and now their relatives are dead. Perfect remains quiet. Sin yells into the phone Perfect are you there? Perfect says; I'm here. Marley is pointing to the ground shaking her head no don't tell her where we are, don't tell her anything. Perfect motions her head up and down okay. Perfect says look Sin I have to go. Sin yells; wait Perfect when you will be home. Perfect says;

I'm not coming home leave me alone don't ever call me again. Sin is still yelling wait wait. Perfect hangs up. Sin makes another call to an associate. Hey I need to know what's going on here on this island where have all the Theirkinds gone. The voice on the other end says; their gone to another island with the revolutionists. Sin says; wait a minute what island what revolutionist? The island is called Promise. It's about a nine hour boat ride from here. Most of the Two Eyes and Three Eyes defected there over a month ago. Sin says; look tell me where this cell phone number was last pinged. The voice gave her the answer in a short while. Ah it was about 800 miles away across the ocean. About the same location as this new island. I'll text you to exact coordination. Sin says; cool okay thanks for the info she hangs up. Sin smiles to herself and says; looks like is time for Sin to pay a visit to Promise she starts to laugh. She goes to her place and packs a bag and then she goes to where her yacht is docked. She boards and sets sail for Promise.

15

Perfect and Cluey meet on Promise

Perfect, Marley, and the babies are finally getting use into their new place. Marley is cooking. Perfect in outside on the front porch watching the babies at play. Being outside was something they would never have been able to do back on Willowiest. Marley joins Perfect on the front porch and they watch the babies play in the front yard. Other children of are all playing together in the front yard. Perfect and Marley laugh at them as they play. Mercy, Grace, and Favor had never seen a beach ball before and the other children are tossing the ball to them and they hold their little hands out to catch the beach balls. Just then Perfect's phone rings she looks at the caller ID its Cluey.

Perfect quickly answers, she yells into her phone with excitement. Cluey! OMG! Where are you? Are you okay? She replies; I'm fine. I left the island. I'm on an island called Promise. My parents and I, packed up what we could, and left Willowiest things were just too crazy there. I just took a chance on calling you. Where are you? Perfect; I'm here on Promise too. Cluey responds; Word! Well shut the front door. We're coming through immigrations now and we should be settled with our new place soon. Perfect's eye grew wide. Oh wow that's great. Cluey asks; but where are you now? We're at our new place, girl you would not believe these houses here, they are absolutely beautiful. It's as though they knew we were coming and it was already prepared for us. They look like mansions. Cluey replies; wow I can't wait. Perfect things are so bad back home. We escaped with our very lives. Where's your parents? Did they come with you? The excitement left Perfect's voice. No they did not come with me. Cluey replies; oh snap for real Per why not? Are they okay? Perfect interrupts; with tears forming in her eye, I don't know, it's a long story I have so much to tell you. Go ahead and get checked in, we'll get together and I'll tell you everything. Cluey replies; okay look I wanna see you girl. I'm calling you back, so we can meet. Perfect replies; okay love you girl. Cluey; love you too. They hang up. Its 5 pm. Perfect and Cluey meet at Perfect's home. They had not laid eyes on one another since all the disruption and chaos that took place back home. Perfect answers the doorbell. They embrace each other. Tears are rolling down the both of their faces. Perfect says; I'm so glad to see you and know you are safe. Cluey replied; girl I'm glad you are safe too. Marley made lunch for them and they all set down to eat. Just then the babies all enter the room and Marley helps place them in their high chairs and they are ready for their lunch too. The babies are suspended in mid-air Cluey face is locked in shock position. Wow how do they do that? Yeah girl you got a lot to tell me about. Is this the voodoo baby I mean the child nut case Nervius was trying to tell me about? Perfect smiles; yeah he's our child me and Nervius. Unfortunately he didn't want anything to do with him. The flying when I first saw it I thought I was losing my mind, it took some getting used too. I have a lot to share with you that I couldn't share before. Cluey interrupts; so that explains you with the baby stroller downtown. Perfect says; yeah that would explain it. But we are here now which I know it was the right move for me I mean for us. Well my father turns out to be truly a horrible piece of work. Cluey bucks her eye; wow really Per? Yes he is. You see this little one right here her name is Grace and this little one his name is Favor. Well turns out they are my half brother and sister. Cluey was stunned; (covering her mouth) OMG for real! Are you kidding me? Perfect responds; no I'm not. Yeah so much for being this up standing law abiding citizen. Oh and it gets better, he came to Marley's house after I poured my guts out to him and my mom. And he turned around and had me followed. Perfect continued with tears rolling down her cheek I believe he was trying to locate by baby to kill him. Cluey's eye continued to grow wider with a big sigh; wow. OMG Girl you have been dealing with a lot.   Per they are so beautiful different as hell but beautiful. Strange but beautiful. Kind of remind me of after I've had a few drinks. I normally don't see anything flying around til then. Perfect laughs; Oh shut up girl. Thank you girl that's just what I needed. I miss your silly self always making me laugh.   And thank goodness for Marley. I don't know what I would have done without her help and guidance. I was so clueless about what was going on with my baby. She helped me so much. I'm not holding anything against my parents, I truly hope that they made it out of there. I haven't heard from them. Cluey says; well all we can do is hope for the best. Perfect asked; How's your parents adjusting to everything over here. Cluey says; girl they're okay over there fussing. My daddy keep saying if my mom keeps getting on his nerves he's gone be outta duct tape and she's gone come up missing. My mom keeps talking about if my dad keeps messing with her, she gone slap him to sleep. Then he says come on and then they are into it. And you know he's got that wooden leg. Why he got it off trying to hit her with it. Then she takes her teeth out and throws it at him. Then he accuse her of trying to put his eye out. He starts crying and tells her that she knows she could have had another baby for him. I'm 20 years old! She keeps telling him she's done and that her eggs are old they're humped over with long grey breads, and how their blind in one eye, and can't see out the other. Then he starts crying. Then they go and lay down together and go to sleep. Get up the next day and it's on again. Dysfunctional ain't even the word. Both of 'em is just crazy as hell. A hot mess. But you know that I love them. I've just learned to keep the knives away from them and let them fuss. Ah Per I've got something to tell you. I ran into Nervius awhile back. Perfect demeanor changes completely a little colder and stiff. Perfect snaps; so you ran into him okay. Cluey continues; I not only ran into him I talk to him. Girl do you know that, that fool rolled up on me with two eyes!! Freaked me out when I saw him! Where they do that at? He texted me after that, said that he was joining the revolution, and he was leaving the island. He told me that he was coming here. That's when I convinced my parents to leave. Perfect replies with a smug look on her face; Oh he did? Cluey says; yes he did. It's a good chance he's here on the island. Perfect said; so what I don't care. I don't want to see him. Cluey replies; he told me something else too. He told me some craziness about you putting a voodoo baby on him, turning him in to a two eyes. I mean seriously? Who does that? I told him that he needed to stop smoking that stuff. Perfect snaps; he's a freakin idiot my baby is not a voodoo baby. Yes as a result of our graduation trip I did have a baby. Not knowing at the time that the idiot man was a two eyes the whole time. Cluey this is why the council was so against everyone mixing for fear of these special babies being born and having more power than they had. What they were too stupid to understand, is that they are powerful, their but harmless. The core of them possess only love. And just think of the things that they could have taught us, but because of their convenient ignorance. It's doesn't matter that there are facts. When there's a klan mentality present the only thing that matters is what the messenger look like and if it's not one of them then the message is not authentic. They would rather here a lie from their kind than the truth proven through video or documentation from another one that is different from them. There must be an oath to go down with the ship no matter what. Hatred is bliss a serious mental trip. Cluey responds; wow Perfect I've never heard you talk this way. It's like you are different or something. Like you are thinking on some kind of different level. Perfect replies; I am I think on a different level. When you bring a child into the world that is different you have too. But it's more than that, taking care of Mercy has opened my mine to what is pure and real. He is a very special baby. Cluey responds; Yeah he is special? Well I saw him and the others float into the room and take a seat. I wasn't going to say anything. But I'm just saying, ah yeah that's special. Perfect begins; well that's not all, as you can see they can fly, they also light up which is their special spiritual light, and with that they can heal you. Cluey looked totally puzzled; WORD! Now that is some kinda different. Perfect continues; but I knew I had to get him out of there, because I knew Mercy and the other were not safe. My dad is one of them that would rather go down with a sinking ship of hatred than to be saved by a floating ship of promise, adventure, and change. Cluey says; Oh Per I'm so sorry I feel like I'm part to blame for what's happened to you. Perfect replies; don't even worry about it, sometimes things that happens to you, have to happen, in order to help reveal other things that we are supposed to do. Like the person I now know my father to be. OMG I'm starting to sound like Marley. And besides, I know Sin put you up to it. That chick is ratchet. Well it's getting late and we'd better turn in. Cluey says; it's going to take some getting used to all this newness and we have to learn our way around this place. It's been a long day, I'm going to get some sleep and I will see you at the meeting in the morning. They embrace again and Cluey goes across the street to her house and Perfect goes inside to her room. Early morning rise, everyone is up and at the town square to be welcomed as new citizens of Promise. There's a parades and the welcome committee to salutes the new citizens with songs and dancers. Right at the end of the celebration. Perfect gets a call she doesn't look at her phone before she answers it. It's Sin she's yelling into the phone; Hey Perfect can you hear me! I'm here! Yeah girl I made it took all night. Perfect covers the phone Marley and Cluey looks on. Perfect says; guys what should I do? She says she's here. Sin still yelling into the phone; hey Perfect girl they ran me out of Willowiest them old farts trying to get their money back. Hey you need to come to the shore and talk to these crazy animals they want let me in! Hey tell them I'm okay! I need to get on this island! I ain't got nowhere to go. Are you there! Perfect and Cluey look at each other and then they look at Marley. Marley is whispering; that girl is bad news, I would not mess with her. Perfect says; you don't have to remind me. Hey yall know she's crazy so maybe, I'll go to the shore, and talk to her hopefully I can get her to go away. Perfect leaves Marley and the babies' at home and her and Cluey heads to the shore. As they were walking on the shore. Cluey stops ask Perfect to sit down for a minute. They sit on the beach. Cluey looks at her best friend says; Perfect you know you are my girl I got to something to tell you. And I don't know where the start. When we were still on Willowiest thing were really getting bad. We got out just in time. There was folks still on the shore waiting. But the police came and started shutting the shores down. So that no one else could leave. And our boat were pulling away, I saw your mom standing on the shore and she saw me. If she had been there seconds earlier I would have put her in the boat with us. But I couldn't we were too far off shore already. Some boats were still leaving. Then the police started shooting at folks. So I don't know if she made it out okay or not. Girl I'm so sorry. I really hope that she made it out okay. I never saw your dad there. Perfect takes her friends hand and says; thank you for telling me this. You know although they never supported me with my baby. I hope that they are okay. I will always love them. Cluey says; girl parents just can be behind the times like that sometimes. Perfect says; we can only hope for the best. The young women stand up and continue their walk to the shore. When they get there they see Sin out in her yacht sitting out 75 yards on the water. She must stay a good distance from the shore of Promise the beast are standing guard at the edge of the shore snarling at Sin's boat. Cluey says; oh snap girl look at that fool out there on the water. Perfect laughs; I know they will not let her on the island. One of the beast spoke to Perfect and Cluey. Do you know this person? Cluey and Perfect says; yes unfortunately we do. She from Willowiest Island. The beast says; her nature is evil and she will not be allowed to come onto the island. Cluey says; oh snap I guess it sucks to be her. She yells out to Sin HATED IT! So there sits Sin in a stupor on her yacht. Arms cross and mad. Sin talking to herself; how dare they deny me entrance. She's yelling from her boat. I'M SIN

HOW COULD YOU DENY ME ENRTY? YOU NEED ME ON THIS ISLAND. She was given a choice she could continue to sit there out on the water or sail away to another place. And every morning Promise was kind enough to send food out, fresh water and fruit to Sin's yacht. Sin is out on her yacht talking to herself. I will find a way to make them accept me.

16

The Escape

Back on Willowiest, totally chaos has erupted on the island, fighting, vandalism, break ins. Economic panic was everywhere with businesses shutting down. Only the rich was left, all the workers were gone. The police had the shores locked down. No one could leave. Patsy comes home. Kilgore is there he's sitting in the living room with a loaded gun in his hand, and he's been drinking. Pasty walks through the door and he draws he's weapon on her. She says put that thing down, it's only me. He says, where have you been? Oh I've been out. He asked have you been trying to leave too. She's watching him with the gun in his hand and she thought better than to say anything about wanting to leave. No ah I had to do some shopping in town. Kilgore starts his rant; well that want be for long the whole island is going to hell in a hand basket. Ungrateful traitors. And where's that brat of ours? Patsy answers; I don't know. I haven't seen our daughter since we refused to help her. Kilgore continues his rant; she broke the law! Patsy turns away from him and says; Kilgore she is still our daughter I don't think we gave her a fair chance. Kilgore laughs; fair chance, we've given her everything. And how does she repay us by having some freakin two eyed brat. And she thought for a minute we would accept it. You got to be kidding me. Besides she broke my law! No one breaks my laws. Patsy turns toward him and says; your laws? Kilgore why don't you put the gun down so we can talk. He starts laughing He says; why do you think I wanna kill you or something. Patsy replies; no you are my husband, I love you. I'm not use to having a conversation with you while you're holding a loaded gun. He makes a staggered shift in his chair. Fine I can put the gun down. He places the gun on the table. She walks over to the table and picks up the gun. She's holding it cross ways of her body with the barrel down. She announces to him; look I love you for whatever that is worth, but I really don't want to be here anymore. I want to go and find our daughter. She needs me. Kilgore interrupts her; she needs you what about me I need you. Patsy ignores his request she continues. I need to get off the island. I'm asking if you can arrange for your goon buddies on the police force to make an exception for me to leave on the boat tonight. I would really like for you to go with me. But I know you want. He peers up at her and says I'm not going anywhere, and neither or you. Patsy remains cool and asked; what do you want me to do here. Nothing is left here but riots and destruction. I don't wanna be here anymore. Kilgore stares at her through his drunkenness. Fine then! Get out go! I give you everything and you're worthless too. Go ahead. Leave then! She places the gun down and slowly walks backwards from the table and then turns and is walking out of the room. Kilgore picks up the gun and points it at the back of her head. She hears him cock the barrel but she keeps walking. Kilgore keeps the gun pointed at the back of her head, his hands are shaking from the booze, he starts to pull the trigger but he doesn't. He puts the gun in his lap and picks up his cell phone and makes a call; hey make sure that your people are on their game tonight. These are my orders shoot to kill anyone that tries to leave this damn island tonight. The voice on the other end says sure thing boss. Patsy heads to the pool house and waits until night fall before going to the shore. Later that night she calls for a taxi. She's waiting at the front of their mansion. As the taxi is pulling up she hears a gunshot go off inside the house. She gets into the taxi and ask him to quickly pull away. He drops her off about a half a block away from the shores. She retrieves a small black suite case from the back seat. As she approaches the shore she positions herself behind an old abandoned beach cottage. She peers out at the shore. It's very dark, all the lights have been cut off. The only light is coming from the moon. In the distance she catch the silhouettes of several police guards positioned on the shore. Just before the shore she see images of others hiding in the brush hoping not to be spotted by police awaiting their escape. There's boats approaching in the distance on the opposite side of the beach away from where the police are stationed. All eyes were on the boats. Theirkinds start moving through the brush to get closer to the rescue boat. Theirkinds are running for the boats. Patsy starts running in the same direction. It's very dark, the police are alerted that there's a boat in the area and they start running in that direction and firing their weapons. Many made it to the boats, but many were falling injured or dead on the beach. Patsy makes it to a boat she was hit several times by the police bullets. She falls inches from the boat but someone pulls her in. They make their escape. The boat sails off but many are left on the shores dead or hurt and many are hurt in the boats. They sail away out to the sea from Willowiest to freedom.

The sun is rising over Promise. A warm tropical breeze continues to blow briskly across the beautiful island. The tides are consistently splashing against the rocks, retreating back out to sea smoothing out the baby blue powder sandy beach. The only sounds were the sea gulls taking flight out over the sea, while the exotic birds were communicating with each other nestled high up in the island trees. Sail boats arrived over night to the shores of Promise. The residence are waking up preparing to go to their welcome parade in town. No one need to make breakfast because everything would be prepared for them down at the square where the festivities would be. Everyone makes their way to the square. There's a stadium that seats ten thousand in attendants. There are many speakers, welcome committees, and entertainment.

Every household received a package that contained everything they needed to know about their new island and their
new homes. The event lasted an hour and everyone dispersed to go home. A watchman greeted the boats arriving to
Promise. The side of the boats read Willowiest Island. There
were Theirkinds inside the boat. They made an announcement anyone of Willowiest Island please come to the shore
immediately. Perfect, Marley, Cluey and the babies heard
the announcement and headed down to the shore. Once at
the shore the watchman cautioned them that this was an ap-
parent attempt to escape from Willowiest and in some of the
boats there was no survivors. There was approximately 20
Theirkinds in the boat. And they needed to know if any of
the decease could be identified. Marley says; you all stay here
I will go. Marley goes over to the boat and looks in. Several
lifeless bloody bodies lying there. She recognizes a woman
it's Perfect's mother she turns and walks away back toward
Perfect. Tears are forming in her eye's she doesn't know what
to say to Perfect. Perfect sees the tears welled up in Marley's
eyes. She starts running toward the boat Marley tries to grab
her, but she breaks free. Perfect reaches the boat she looks
into the boat and falls to her knees screaming mom No! No!
Not my mom no! Marley and Cluey get on their knees close
to her trying to console her. Perfect is crying and saying; it's
all my fault. She tried to follow me. I'm to blame for this!
She takes her mother's lifeless hand and talks to her. Mom
mom wake up! I'm so sorry forgive me. Please forgive me.
Mercy, Grace, and Favor are hovering the boat in midair. At
that moment Favor lands on Patsy's chest and he places his

little hand over her heart. They don't understand. Favor begins to glow and everyone looks on. The shadow of death lifts from Patsy's face her color returns the blood stained wounds starts to dry up then they disappear. Her heart starts to beat again. Perfect is still holding her hand, her fingers start to move within Perfect's hand. Perfect raises her head and looks at her mother Patsy's eye opens. Favor lifts off her chest. She is alive again. Patsy sits up in the boat. Perfect is still holding her hand. She lets out a sigh of relief Oh mom Oh mom. She helps her out of the boat and hugs her tight. Favor lands on another person inside the boat. Until all the dead in the boats were alive again. Perfect tearful but relieved holds on to her mother's hand; Mom I'm so glad you're here with me. I love you and I need you so much. We need you. Mercy comes over and lands gently in his mother's arms. Patsy looks at Mercy he is smiling at her and she smiles back at him. Perfect says tearfully; Mom I want you to come home with us. And I would like for you to meet your grandson Mercy. Then she turns to Mercy and says Mercy I would like you to meet your grandma. Patsy says; it's very nice to meet you Mercy. Before Perfect can finish her sentence. Mercy stretches his little arms out reaching for Patsy to take him. Patsy smiles and takes him into her arms and cuddles him close. He gives her a big loving hug.

17

Nervius experience on Promise

As Nervius was making his way through the crowd to go home. He remembers what happened to him, at Marley's house. He kept half of his face covered with a scarf to hide himself. But little did he know, the tragedy that scared him and the transformation that changed him, would be the blessing that would position him into being the leader he was meant to be. A life coach named Ben spots Nervius and his scarf in the crowd and decided to approach him. Hi my friend my name is Ben. And yours? Hi my name is Nervius. They exchange a friendly hand shake. It's nice to meet you. How long have you been here on the island? Nervius responds a few months ah I was actually one of the first to come here. Ben asked. Did you come over from Willowiest? Yeah I did. Ben says; yeah me and my wife we came over a few weeks ago. We came over from Jessup. It was nice there but we really like it here. Everyone is so nice and friendly. You know you're really in a good place don't you. Nervius responds; yeah I suppose. You don't think so? Nervius responds you wouldn't understand it if I told you. Ben gives him a big smile try me. I might you never know. Nervius starts; well I was living a pretty good life back on Willowiest, until something happened to me, and now everything has changed like you would not believe. I'm not sure what am supposed to do here. What's expected of me and can I cut it. Ben looks at Nervius worried face. Oh my friend I beg to differ. Everybody here is successful. No matter what your story is. You have everything you need free and clear. So what's the worry? Can I let you in on something? Everyone here came from trouble. Places they can't return to. But they were appointed to be here. And you my friend were selected to be here too. Nervius responds, selected by who? Ben says, the one that controls our destiny. He who rules by day and night. He who govern the seas. He's the beginning and the ending of time. He who made you and me. And everything else in the world. Nervius asked, so what does He want from us? Ben says; He wants our belief, our love, our worship, and our faith in Him. All for the glory of Him. He's given us everything else. See once you are here you can never go back to where you came from, or back to who you use to be. This place was not designed for that. Death doesn't live here. Everyone you see here, from the moment their feet touched the blue sand, they became new creatures in Him. And tell me this? Since you've been here have you seen anyone pay for anything? Nervius says no. Since you've been here, have you seen any signs posted to buy, purchase, or sell anything? Nervius replies no. Ben continues. And you never will. Out of the bondage of injustice, you were chosen to come to here. Besides the only thing that awaited you in Willowiest is destruction. Who cares to live in a world that judges you, socially divides you, discriminates against you, by what you look like, by how much you earn, and what you own. Then they get to tell you who you can or cannot socialize with, who you can and cannot love, who you can and cannot marry. My friend any society that is divided by status, breeds bigotry, hatred, and a false sense of entitlements. Not even the ones that most benefit from this type of living are happy. Because they are constantly doing a check and balance of their happiness and unhappiness. So no one can could be truly happy living in an environment like that. So let's strap that status idea. Now can I ask you to trust me? Nervius says yes. Ben continues, I just want you to see what I see. I need you to trust me take that silly scarf off your face. Why are you hiding who you are? No one is here to judge you. This is not you. You don't need it. You are hiding your true identity. Come on my friend trust it. Nervius takes a big swallow, looks at Ben, and reluctantly removes the scarf from his face. Ben continues talking to him, see now that's got to feel better. Look around and take in the view. Man don't block your blessings looking back. Nervius really tries hard see the beauty through Ben's eyes. But the eye that he's hidden for so long is not yet clear.

Ben continues coaching him; see now not only do you have sight but vision too. The more he blinked the clearer the eye became. It was his spiritual eye. And he did began to see. Love, peace, and joy. No worries about money, prestige, and status was important to him. The tropical breeze blowing across the island spanked his face. As the wind blew he could hear a very faint voice calling him. There was a peace with him that he had never experienced before. He thanked his friend and he went about his way. Ben reminded him of the town hall meeting that they were having tonight. Nervius assured him that he would be there. He said good bye to Ben and began walking in the direction of the voice. He came upon a hillside, the voice instructed him to rest there. It was so inviting he climbed to the top of it. Once on top there was a field of soft beautiful yellow grass. He laid down and the grass nestled around his body. Nervius says to himself wow I'm so sleepy. This is so comfortable I don't understand it and he drifts off into a peaceful sleep. He can still hear the voice talking to him. MY SON COME TAKE YOUR REST FOR I'VE BEEN WAITING FOR YOU. Nervius asked; who are you? The voice responds I AM YOUR HOLY CREATOR. Nervius asked; what is your name? I AM THAT I AM. Nervius asked; why am I here. The voice responds; I HAVE CHOOSEN YOU TO BE A LEADER OVER MY PEOPLE. Nervius says; I don't know if I can so much has happened to me. How can I know that I'm ready? The voice replies; BECAUSE I ALLOWED THOSE THINGS TO HAPPEN TO STRENGTHEN YOU FOR THIS APPOINT TIME. THE SCAR ON YOUR FACE I HAVE HEALED WITH

MERCY. THE SCARS IN YOUR HEART AND MINE I WILL ERASE WITH LOVE. YOUR ROLE IS TO BE A MIGHTY WORRIOR, A GOOD HUSBAND, AND A GOOD FATHER. Nervius respond; But who am I to do this? I have done so much wrong. My best friend is dead because of me, I had a baby outside of marriage, and the mother of my child hates me. I've worshiped money. Why would you still choose me after all of that? THE VOICE RESPONDS; ONLY THOSE THAT I TRULY LOVE DO I CHASTISE. YOU'RE HEART AND DETERMINATION HAS CHOOEN YOU FOR SUCH A TASK. LOVE ME FIRST AND YOU WILL BE LOVED BECAUSE OF ME. I'VE RESTORTED EVERYTHING IN YOU THAT WAS TAKEN FROM YOU. MY SON I HAVE DONE A NEW THING IN YOU. FOR THE OLD MAN THAT LIED DOWN HAS DIED AND THE NEW MAN THAT WILL GET UP AND HE SHALL LIVE FOREVER IN MY PURPOSE. YOU WILL NOW SEE THE SIGNS THAT YOU NEED TO SEE. FEEL THE THINGS THAT YOU NEED TO FEEL. LOVE BEYOND ALL PETTINESS IN MY NAME. KNOW THAT MY YOKE IS EASY AND MY BURDEN IS LIGHT. NOW GO. FOR I WILL BE WITH YOU ALWAYS. Nervius awaken a few hours later. He sat up in the field, he noticed just over his left shoulder. A little dark cloud with lightening and rain coming down from it. He took his right hand and tried to brush it away. It quickly disappeared then reappeared. He looked over his right shoulder and it was a tiny sun with beautiful sun rays all around it. He brushed at it and he's hand went through it, it did not go away. He shook his head and blinked eyes, but both was still there. Feeling refreshed he remembered the dream of the Higher One speaking to him. He remembered everything. He took a moment, looking around him, his sight was clear his vision was better. He saw peace, calm, and joy. His heart was no longer heavy. He remembered the town hall meeting, he got up and took off toward the square. As he arrived they were just starting. He spotted his friend Ben. They took seats together in the stands. There were many speakers, with very uplifting messages, some instructional, some very spiritual. After the meeting Ben and Nervius was walking from the meeting headed for the cafe. Ben said you know my friend there's nothing greater than love. Nervius looked at him and asked; why do you say that? Ben says; well it's so powerful it can break a heart or change a world. I know you've had to have loved someone in your life. Right? Nervius responds; well beyond loving my folks I haven't been too successful at it. Ben said, surely not, come on now you've had to have something good to happen. Nervius looked worried well sort of kinda. Ben said come on now don't shut me out. We're supposed to be friends. Nervius looks at him sadly, I had this person that ah, well we ended up conceiving a child together. But she kinda hates me right now. I don't even know if they made it here. She hasn't answered any of my calls. That is about as close as to anything I've had to love. Ben looked at Nervius and smiled. You have a child? Nervius responds; yeah I do but it's a lot more complicated. Ben smiles again. You are so blessed to have an offspring. The misses and I have been trying for a while. Nervius said with his head down, reluctantly thank you. Ben asked, what's that matter? Well we weren't married. I admit that I did not receive the situation all that well. I only found out after she actually had the baby. I was there believe me it wasn't planned. It took both of us by surprise. She didn't realize she was having a baby until it was born on the floor of her apartment. I was with her when it happened. Ben's eyes grew wide with a wow expression. But I guess I don't get any credit for that. The baby is a two eyes. Like me. He's quite special. Ben asked; what do you mean by special? Nervius said, well it's a long story you and probably wouldn't believe me if I told you. I didn't mind being there for her though. She just kept pushing the situation on me. And it was all I could do to get my head around even having a child. I really hope they made it here. She really was a pretty decent person too. Just frustrated by her circumstances. I never really told her but I do care for her. And now that my eyes are more open. I want to be in my son's life as well. I where ever they are hope they are all right. Ben placed his arm around Nervius's shoulder, well my friend, we are going to stay positive, hope for the best for them, and hope that they did make it here. Tell you what, we're are going to our first committee meeting. Nervius asked; what is that about? So everyone will know what's available to them here on the island different service and so forth. This is so we can be united equally as an island. All homes are beautiful spacious, all are 4000 square feet, and they are all the same. Everyone will shop at the same free stores. Go to the same events, worship in the same synagogues. No division because of some silly law labeling folks by the number of eyes or anything foolish like that. They got their meal and proceeded on to the town square where the meeting was held. Everyone is at the square. The speakers took the stages. They elected all groups of government. And each one consisted of a One eye because of their expertise in economic financial growth, a Two eyes because of their talents and sense of community, and a Three eyes because of their sense of humanity, vision, and spiritual insight. When all was said and done. Their new government was formed of a very diverse coalition. For all Theirkinds, by all Theirkinds. After the last speaker, there was a closing prayer for the crowd, everyone dispersed and began going home. As Nervius stood up he saw a glimpse of a woman that caught his eye. It was Marley. He remembered her. He jumped to his feet, made his way through the crowd, toward her. He called to her. Not remembering her name he's yelling Ma'am ma'am! Hey wait a minute! Marley has Grace and Favor in their stroller waiting for Perfect, she turns and sees him rushing toward her. He finally reaches her he's out of breath. He's smiling so you made it. Marley smiles and says yes we did. Nervius asked; we? Marley cuts him off. Yes she made it too and so did your son. Just then Perfect emerged from the restroom with Mercy in her arms. She see Nervius. She looks at him with a smug look on her face. Well hi Nervius I see you made it here. Nervius looks at her. Yes I did. And I'm glad to see you that you all made it here too. I'm really glad you both made it here safe. Mercy reaches for Nervius from Perfect's arms, beckoning for his dad to take him. Perfect backs up and was reluctant at first, but she allows him to go to his dad. He takes his son, looks at

him and smiles. He holds his son up and says; hey little fellow, I'm your dad no turning me into a frog or anything.
Marley walks away to give them some privacy. She says I'll be
over here.   Nervius starts Per can I ask you something?
Perfect says, what? Nervius says, ah do you see anything over
my left shoulder. Perfect says, no why? Nervius says, never
mind. Perfect says, well this is a switch act like you're actually
glad to see us? And don't call me Per. Only my real friends
can call me that. You just up and left the island and never
bothered to call or let us know anything. Nervius responds; I
had no choice. They threw us in jail, drugged us all, then put
us on boats and pushed us out to sea to die. But we didn't die.
I've been here ever since. Look Perfect, all that stuff that
happened at the baby sitters that night really messed me up. I
had to leave to find myself again. I had to learn who I was.
How could I be anything to you or this child if I didn't even
know who I was? So I came here. And I'm still learning myself. I had no life left back there but I do now. I couldn't make
the money I needed to make as a two eye's if I tried. He looks
at Mercy and Mercy smiles at him. He look into his baby's
face and smiles back at him. And for the first time he actually
enjoys looking at his son. He looks at Perfect and he can see
the anger and bitterness she has toward him. And Mercy begins cooing in his arms and Nervius starts talking to his son
again. The uneasiness in Perfect's face is replaced by a confusion, she was seeing something from him, she had never
seen before. He was actually engaging with their child. A
man only a few months back wanted nothing to do with their
baby. Perfect snaps at him. What are you doing? Nervius

looks at her. Perfect what do you mean? I playing with my son. Perfect turns her face slightly to the side and squints her eye at him. She doesn't trust what she's seeing, how he is acting toward Mercy. . He slowly rocks him back and forth in his arms. And Mercy is loving it. Yeah this is dad's little special guy. Perfect if it would be okay I would like to talk to you later when there's not so many people around. Perfect quickly ask; Talk about what? He responds; about stuff. Perfect says; I really don't have time. Remember? I have a child to raise by myself. Nervius asked; please think about it. Perfect says; I have to go now. I have to get Mercy home and down for a nap. I'll think about it. They went their separate ways in the crowd

Perfect, Marley, and Patsy are in the living room watching TV. Patsy comes and sat down beside Perfect and takes her hand. Tears are rolling down Patsy's face she begins. Honey I would like to apologize to you for everything that happened back on Willowiest. I didn't understand everything that was going on myself. Perfect interrupts; you mean about dad. Patsy responds; yes. I knew your father was dealing with some shady stuff, I just did not know how shady. I guess I just didn't want to realize the truth about him. In spite of it all I do still love him. I hope he is okay. But I have to ask you, can you ever forgive me for not being on your side, not defending you when you needed me too. I'm so sorry honey. But you had to admit after all it did sound so bizarre. Perfect responds. Mom that's okay you didn't understand even the type of man dad was. I understand that you could not have comprehended all of this. And you're my mom, of course I forgive you. They gave each other a strong hug. Perfect said; let's forget about it okay. Patsy responds; okay. Their having their usual after dinner tea. At that moment Perfect phone lights up buzzing with a tune. It's Nervius. She looks at the phone trying to decide to take the call, she does. Nervius; Hi what are you doing? Perfect answers his question coldly, I just put the babies down for the night and Marley, my mom, and I are having some tea. What do you want? Nervius ah I'd like to meet with you tomorrow if it's okay. Perfect snaps; for what? Nervius; Oh come on Per. She snaps at him again, don't call me Per. That's what my real friends call me. Nervius keeps trying; Perfect will you meet with me tomorrow please. Perfect; I will think about it and let you know. Good night. She hangs up the phone. Marley asks, Ms. Perfect it's only 5 O'clock honey don't you even want to hear what he has to say? Perfect; no not really. When we were back on Willowiest he treated Mercy awful. Marley responds, yes honey, but I think that was out of fear. And besides, he could have denied his involvement and told on you but he didn't. He kept it a secret. Perfect looks at Marley. You always see the good in everybody don't you? Marley smiles at her I try too. So you'll meet with him? Yes I will. The next morning, Perfect calls Nervius's. She's still very guarded about her feelings. She starts the conversation. Hi, he says ah hi. What is so urgent that you want to talk to me about? Nervius bracing for rejection takes along swallow. If you don't mind. I would like to talk to you face to face. Will you meet me at the café at the town square this afternoon? Perfect snaps, and why would I do that? Because I wanna see you and I wanna to talk to you about something. Ah, about us. Perfect looks confused. She responds back, us? What us? What are you referring too? Nervius starts again, please Perfect I just wanna sit down and talk with you, and after that hey if you don't ever wanna see to me again, then that's find. Perfect is really playing hard to get but agrees to meet with him. Let's meet at 1pm today. As planned they meet at the town square café. Perfect walks in Nervius already has a table for them. It's a cozy little corner booth, so they can have the most privacy. She sees him in the corner beckoning her to come over. She walks over arms folded and takes a seat. Nervius starts, Perfect I asked you to meet with me today, because I would like to talk to you about our situation. Perfect cuts him off. You mean our child. He says yes. She cuts him off again. He is not a situation. He is a baby that deserves to be loved. Nervius jumps back in the conversation. Now Perfect I didn't mean it that way. I know he does. I know he is just not a situation he is our child. But please just here me out. I wanted to take this moment and apologize to you from the depths of my heart. I was totally wrong, stupid and scared. Perfect says; so far you're right. Nervius continues; and not only am I here to talk about him but also about us. Perfect cuts him off again. And I repeat us? What us? He closed his eyes, says to himself for a moment, this is not going to be easy, stay focused and remember your connection with the Holy One. He said a good father and a good husband. Perfect I want this work for us as a family. There's nothing like the love of a family. I'm at a different place now. I see things differently I feel different, happier inside and out. We are at a good place and we never got to deal with this beyond the point of you just bringing the baby into the world. Perfect I'm talking about doing things right with you. I'm talking about us, trying to build something. A relationship with you. Perfect stares at him for a moment before saying anything. Then she starts. Nervius we can't just decide because we had a child together, that we are going to work. Not long ago you were talking about putting one of our baby's eyes out or worst killing him. He interrupts her. Perfect I know I know I did. And that was stupid of me, I was just scared, and I should have never said those things. But I'm not that guy anymore. I'm very so sorry for that. Can you ever forgive me for that? She looks at him in disbelief. What's happened to you? You've changed. Are you smoking that Sash again? No Perfect come on. I'm for real. Can you please forgive me? I'll get on my knees if I have too. He jumps down on the floor yelling in the restraurant making a scene. Whatever it takes to make this right between us, I'll do it! I was stupid and blind at the same time! Just say you forgive Per come on! Perfect just looks at him. Get up you nut case you're embarrassing me. I forgive you. Nervius shouts; you do? he leaps to his feet and runs around to her side of the booth, grabbed her up in a big embrace, and kissed her right on the lips. Perfect was stunned and intrigued all at the same time. She yelled, Nervius what are you doing? The moment he realized what he had done, he sprang back from her, his palms back. Oh crap, I'm so sorry I'm so sorry, I was just excited. He knew exactly what he was doing. I over reacted. I meant to say thank you thank you for forgiving me. Perfect stood up and said well I need to be getting back. I have to get Mercy a bath and help Marley get the other little ones down for a nap. This it was interesting. But I have to go now. He takes her hand. Hey Per wait. Look I'm serious about us at least trying to see if we can make a go at this. Just you and me. He smiles and baby makes three. Promise me you will at least think about it. Perfect looks at him in the eyes I promise she would think about it. She starts to walk away. He stops her again Hey Perfect if it's not asking too much or being to forward. Can I have another hug this time no kissing, I promise she agrees, they embrace for about 4 seconds long. Perfect enjoys the embrace, he smells so good. Besides her father, she had never been hugged by a man especially like that for that long. Of course he wasn't hugging her like a father he was hugging her like a man. He says look I'm going to be calling you very soon. Please pick up your phone. She promised she would. They say good bye and parted ways each to their own dwellings.

18

Precious Steps

Over the next few months, Nervius and Perfect laid their difference aside, for the sake of their child, and took steps to develop a new friendship and a real bond as parents to raise their child together. As the months passed, they were seen together a lot, especially at socials events, eating out, church, and at the playground with Mercy. One day, while at the playground, a young boy fell off the swing set and skinned his knee, he was crying and his mother along with others rushed to his side. Now a one year and a half old Mercy walks over to where the young boy was held his hand and the scrap knee healed immediately. Mercy then gave him a big hug. The mother was so happy, she said he is so precious, to do that for my child. Perfect and Nervius stood there smiling as proud parents. As time passed, the babies' powers became stronger and as time went by Perfect and Nervius became closer enjoying each other's company. Nervius visited his secret hillside many times to learn from the Holy One as to how he should be as a man. To better his self and it began to show in his attitude. One day Nervius came over to take Perfect out. Mercy stayed home with Marley. They walked all over the island and Nervius decided to take her to his special place. He said to her. This is where I spend a lot of time when I need answers to questions about my life that is important for me to know. He climbed up on the hillside, spread out a large blanket. He stretches out his hand and invited Perfect to join him on the hillside. Perfect looks at him hesitantly, takes his hand, and joined him on the hillside. They're lying there side by side they as first say nothing to each other. They enjoy the softness of the grass, which messages them beneath the blanket. Then Nervius reaches over and takes her hand. She doesn't resist he starts to talk to her. Hey Perfect I know a lot has happened over the past months. And I really feel that we have developed a good relationship with one another. We are at different place now. All the troubles of Willowiest are behind us. Perfect nods her head to agree. I mean I know all this change has been hard on you because it's been hard on me too. You know adjusting to a new place and all. Perfect stops him, ah Nervius where is this going. He starts again, well at first, I thought I would never be able to say this, but now that I've had an opportunity to get to spend time with my son, I mean our son, and get to know him and he's gotten to know me. I love him very much. Perfect says, Nervius so why are you saying all of this? He says, I guess what I'm saying is that we should be doing the right thing as parents and responsible adults. We have a child, I've always thought you were a good person. I wanna do the right thing as a father. Perfect asks, Nervius what does that mean? Nervius says; I love you Perfect, I think we should be married, so I can be the good husband you need, and be a good father to Mercy that he needs. Perfect's mouth flew open. She sits up on the blanket. He sits up too starring at her waiting for a response. Nervius looks at her waiting for a response. She starts, Nervius I am flattered that you would think of me that way. But I have to ask. Do you want to marry me because we have a baby or do you want to marry me because you truly love me?

He responds, all of the above. Perfect it is a blessing to be married, it's a blessing to be married with a child. So there are no wrong answers here. Perfect I enjoy watching the way you care for Mercy. Making sure he's every need is met. That makes me happy. He gets up and helps her to stand up. Then he gets back down on one knee. Tell you what, he reaches in his pocket, and pulls out a small box. He opens it there's a beautiful 2k platinum diamond ring is inside. He takes the ring and places it on her finger. Perfect I am the only man you have ever been with. I am all the man you need. Perfect I love you will you marry me. She stares at him in disbelief. She starts to speak. He stops her. He says, if you need time I will understand. If you're feeling some kind of way you don't have to answer that right now. I want you to go home and think about it. So that you will have time to search your heart and make your decision from your heart. Perfect agreed that she would. As they walked back toward Perfect's place she kept stealing peeks at the beautiful ring he had placed on her finger. And she would then look at Nervius which really in her view had changed for the better. Being there for Mercy trying to be the best father he knew how to be. Everything he said to her was true. They finally reached her front door step and she wished him a good night he took her hand and squeezed it gently and left. She wished that he had kissed her but she accepted the hand holding. Once inside everyone was asleep. She retires to her room, showers and change for bed. Once in bed she kept replaying all the events of the night in her head. She had a lot to think about. As a man should do he made his intentions clear to me. He wants to marry me for all the right reasons. What do I have to loose. Nothing. What do I have to gain? Everything. On that notes she drifts off to sleep. The next morning Perfect awakes with last evening's events still on her mind. Things floating around in her head. She's thinking t herself. Wow marriage? This is a big step. Can anyone really change that much? He really acts like he has changed. Just then her mom knocks on her door and calls out to her. Perfect honey breakfast is ready. She responds back oh okay mom. Her mother then opens the door. Honey are you alright? Perfect sits up in her bed staring at the ring Nervius put on her finger the night before. Patsy walks in honey what's the matter. Mom can we talk for a minute. Her mom comes in and takes a seat on her bed. What is it honey? She shows Patsy the ring on her finger. Her mother gasped, he proposed to you? Perfect says yes he did. Patsy asked and you said yes? No mom I didn't. Patsy pressed further do you love him? I've always loved him as a friend but I always knew in my heart that it could be more. Because Nervius is a good guy. He could have ruined me back on Willowiest and he didn't. Even when Mercy changed him he kept quiet. And I understand when he was mad at me. It was because he was scared and I must admit, I did push this on him. But what I have to realize because of Sin we created this child. But now because of love we can raise this child. And he feels that we must be correct before the Holy One so we can be blessed. Last night he told me not to give him an answer, but to go home and think about it. Mom I don't want him to marry me out of pity. I want him to marry me because he feels truly in his heart I am the one. Her mother takes her hand. Baby did he tell you that he felt sorry for you or did he say he loved you. Perfect replies, he said that he loved me. Then baby that is your answer. Are you afraid? A little. Her mother sat closer to her and put her arms around her and said oh sweetie that is so normal to be a little afraid. But follow your heart and it will always lead you the right way. Now come on and let's get some breakfast. They get up and head to the kitchen. Marley the babies and Ms. Likey are all seated at the table. Everyone says their good mornings. Perfect shows off her beautiful new diamond engagement ring. Ms. Likey perks up FOR BETTER OR FOR WORST FOR BETTER OR FOR WORST FOR BETTER OR FOR WORST. THIS IS BETTER YOU CAN DO WORST. And they all burst out laughing Perfect goes over to Ms. Likey and gives her a big hug. Just then there's a knock at the door. Patsy goes to the

door and answers it. Its two young ladies a Two eye's and a
Three eyes. They ask, is Ms. Marley here? Patsy says yes. She
doesn't invite them in she gets Marley to come to the door.
Marley comes to the door and says Oh my goodness! Please
come in. She gives them a big hug. It's the mothers of Grace
and Favor. All three are crying. Perfect, Patsy, and Ms. Likey
looks on with anticipation. Marley turns and introduce the
young women. Everyone I would like you to meet Grace and
Favor's moms'. Everyone gasp, in surprise. Marley explains,
I'm crying because I thought something happened. They all
gather around the breakfast table and. One of the young
women went on to explain. We left Willowiest shortly after
the boat started arriving at night. We knew our lives were in
danger and we had no choice but to leave or be killed. And
we've been living here on Promise ever since. We heard about
all the destruction going on back on Willowiest and prayed
that Ms. Marley got out with our babies. We heard that you
made it here to the island and decided to look for you. So we
found out through the registry office and they gave us your
address. The young women faces lite up when they saw their
babies. They began crying and immediately ran over to where
their babies were seated and picked them up and embraced
them in a big hug. Now we don't have to be afraid to have our
babies with us anymore, we came to take them home with us.
Marley smiled at them and said I totally understand. I'll go
and pack their things. So Marley and Patsy packed up all the
baby's things and they all give tearful hugs and off they went
with their children. Perfect made them promise to bring the
children over to play with Mercy. Perfect calls Nervius and

ask if they can meet for lunch. He agrees, they meet at a small café in town. Perfect is already inside, seated at a table. Nervius walks in, he sees her, she looks very nervous. He joins her he says; Hi..................she says Hi Perfect starts, well you know you asked me to give your proposal some thought. And I have, I've concluded that marriage is a big step. You know it's like for better or worst. And til death do we part? Let me ask you something and he looks stress but he listens. She ask, why didn't you turn me in to the authorities back on Willowiest. He responds, Perfect you really don't know? She looks at him. Know I don't. Perfect I wouldn't have turned you in even if Mercy was not mind. Because I knew what happened to you, to us was not your fault. It was Sin. I watched you in College, you were a good girl. And you still are. Actually, I kinda fell for you from a far. But I never told anyone. I watched the way you carried yourself. The other girls were nice and some were fresh. But you were always the same. Honest, sweet, and wholesome. That's what men like in Theirkind women. Perfect's face was frozen at this new flattering information. Nervius cuts her off. If you're scared? Then say you're scared. But don't make up excuses. I'm scared too but we can be scared together. Perfect replies; so what if I am scared but I still want to that chance with you. Nervius didn't hear her he continues talking. Per Because of Sin we conceived a child. Let's not let fear keep us from raising our child I know it's a big step, and I know you're scared, so am I. But I know you are the right one. Finally he heard her, Nervius bucked his eyes in surprise...he stopped talking mid-sentence. I know that we can......... What did you just

say? You wanna take a chance with......She cuts him off, yes I
do. Our son needs a father, you, his father. I don't want another man raising our son. And I need you in our lives. And
you need us in your life as well. Nervius is overwhelmed with
joy. He leaps up from his side of the table runs around to her
side and gives her a big huge. As he's clutching his arms
around her, he says. Look around us we have everything we
need. We are new. Our start is new. I know this is right. Let's
make this right. So now Perfect I ask you again, will you marry me? She looks at him with a big smile on her face. And says
yes I will. Two months later there's a beautiful setting in the
town square. Celebrating the first wedding on the island.
Perfect and Nervius were married at The Heavenly chapel
Inn on Promise. There were bands playing, dancing and
singing, her dress was snow white, the train of her vail was
12ft. long, they ate and celebrated until dawn. All of Promise
attended. Six months later life had settled in for the happy
couple. A very pregnant Perfect set out on the porch watching her baby Mercy play with his little friends. He is 1 1/2
years old now and walking and playing with his friends Grace
and Favor. Meanwhile back on Willowiest Island.

19

The Attack on Promise

As months went by the economy of Willowiest declined all the lower class and the poor were gone. Trade deals went flat because there were no workers to gather their crops. All the little affluent One eyed children had to stay home because all of their day cares and schools closed because all of the teachers were gone. No fisherman, restaurant servers, no cooks, no dishwashers, no hair dressers, no bus drivers, stores were closing because there were no customers. The stench rose high in the great homes of the One eyes because there were no maids or butlers to clean up their filth. Some One eyes had to set home they never learned to drive because there were no chauffeurs.

Kilgore and the councilmen of Willowiest called a meeting in their war room. Several member was in favor to wage war on Promise. And so they devised a plan of attack. One shouted; they think they have gotten away from us but we have only just begun to fight. Our plan must be solid and our attack against them must be strong. Kilgore their leader took the stand. I have an idea. We have satellites don't we. They have a satellites too. Well we will design a virus of despair send it through their airways and mess them up good. It want be paradise for long. He starts laughing the whole room lit up in laughter and cheers. They put some of their best heads together to come up with this diabolical virus to unleash on the Island of Promise. Their IT guy explained see we can use this technology to attack their airways, a cyber-attack, they want know what hit them. The crowd cheered. Kilgore said lets be specific about this so called cyber-attack; what do you mean? We have satellites and they have satellites right? We can upload a virus that will be released in the air that will cause them to act out with confusion and madness, all generated through the airways, they want know what hit them. And the councilmen put their greatest technical minds on the island to work and devised a virus and entered it through their computer system and upload it to their satellites. Then they turned their satellite toward Promise and with a click of a button their rays of confusion, madness, unnatural behavior was traveling through the airways to its intended target. People on Promise were working and shopping commuting, laughing, singing, eating lunch together, playing at the park, then suddenly a flash over the island sparked, and fights broke out pushing and shoving, stealing, Theirkinds started throwing bricks and smashing windows in buildings and store fronts. Theirkinds were fighting, choking each other, cursing, screaming and yelling at each other, this was happening all over Promise. This behavior went on for 3 days. As they were trying to maintain control of the island, they were in the square witnessing all sorts of destructive behavior that surrounded them. Nervius, Ben, and the other leaders did not understand what was happening. This would continue for 3 days. Finally Nervius and the other leaders met to see if they could figure out what was going on. They tested the water, the food, the soaps, perfumes, they found nothing. Finally they tested their satellites and they found that there had been a virus of some kind loaded in their system. They discovered that it came from Willowiest Island. They quickly counter acted the virus killing it from their system. And the citizens all returned to normal. They called their first war room meeting to seek revenge on Willowiest Island. Nervius took the stand. Brethren's we have been secretly attacked through our satellites by Willowiest Island. This is what have caused our people to act unusual. This means war! I strongly suggest that we give them back a taste of their own medicine. We need to devise a plan of attack to get them back for what they have done to us. But it needs to be such a plan that it will send a message to them that they will never forget and they will think twice before ever attacking us again. But rest assure we found a way to counteract their attack. The leaders suggested from now on we set up meditation tents all around the island to keep away all evil attacks against them.

But we must not allow them to get away with this attack. We must retaliate, we must let them know that we are not afraid to fight back and the same tactics they use on us we will use on them. So they devised their plan they would use their same virus but on a more vicious scale. Not only did the virus included confusion and madness it included fear, hallucinations, hatred, thievery, and murder. It would suspend all of their cell phones. And we will wait until midnight so it will be a surprise attack and take affect overnight. And so they did, that night, they returned the favor to Willowiest and turned their satellite on them. With one click of a button the virus was sent. At first light, the citizens of Willowiest awakened to the sounds alarms. People yelling and screaming on the streets, chaos was amassed everywhere. Glass breaking, fighting and cursing. The councilmen were still inside their homes. They did not know what was going on. They were trying to call one another but the phone lines were jammed. They tried to call the town's police to see what was going but all of their communications were down. Just in that moment the lead councilman heard a pounding knock on his door. He went and peeped out of his peep hole it was his second in command council leader. He quickly opened the door, he rushed in. Man it is insane out there. Theirkinds on Willowiest had gone mad. Looting and car accidents everywhere. What in the hell happened. The leader looks at him and said you know what has happened. They did to us what we did to them. We just didn't know that they would find out so soon what we did to them. The second in command says; what are we going to do? They're going mad out there. I wonder how they recovered in such a quick time to return the favor to us. Man it's not safe out there. The leader said; look you made it over here, I need you to gather as many of our members together as possible. Before he could finish his sentence another frantic knock came to the door. The leader ran and looked out the peep hole it was another council member. He opened the door the member and he fell into his arms. He said; it's a mad house out there look they just took my whole family out everybody is dead, I had to play dead until they left, we've got to do something. With his last breath, he died in the leaders arms. He laid his limp body on the floor. He looked at the second leader in command and said; this is war Promise has just drew blood. We have to find as many members as possible if their still alive and devise a plan to blow Promise off the map. Out of 1500 members there were only 300 of them that were still alive. They Kilgore's house. To devise their plan attack. They decided that they would use their satellites again but this time they would do all they can to destroy Promise. They devised a nas- ty weather virus to first send first as a beautiful sun and then it would turn into a dark rain cloud and then rain drops would turn into fire with burning spears would falling from the sky on Promise. They uploaded their weather virus to all ten of their satellites and waited until midnight as the Theirkinds on Promise slept, to release their attack. But what they did not know Promise had put in a cyber-alarm system to detect anything coming through their airways. And they had increase the activity of their meditation and prayer camps to 24 hours a day. That completely surrounded their island. Giving them spiritual protection. But as mid-night came Willowiest leaders sent their weather virus through the airways. The alarms went off, citizens of Promise leaped from their beds, awakened by the alarm. At first a beautiful sun moved over the island. Nervius was awakened by the alarm. The citizens were awaken and everyone went outside. They were amazed to see such a beautiful sun at night over their island. But Nervius remembered that he had a tiny sun that appeared over his right should and he could not understand why it was there. Just then he remembered that he was that after the Holy spoke to him. He started yell-ing at everyone to get back this was not good get back now. The beautiful sun quickly turned into a fierce monstrous black cloud hovering over the tiny island of Promise. Rolling with thunder, and flashes of lighting shooting throughout the clouds, and it begin to rain. Everyone was outside look-ing up into the sky. Nervius pointed to the sky and said I know that cloud it is the same one that kept appearing over my shoulder. It was a sign of things to come. Everyone take cover. And the citizens of Promise took cover. Perfect, Marley, Cluey, and all the babies were outside looking up at all the commotion going on above them. The meditation and prayer camps had been in place praying night and day. They heard the alarms sound, and they started praying louder and louder. And as the rain fell it did reach the island, the prayers became stronger. Just then Mercy, Grace, and Favor took flight from the arms of Perfect and Marley, in the air toward the storm. Perfect and Marley was screaming for them to come back. Their little tiny bodies formed a protective barrier of light over the island, like a bubble. The rain fell harder and began to turn into fire and spears. And all the beasts in fields, began to wail at the mountainside. And the three great beasts appeared, the Father, the Son, and the Spirit. The great beast saw the dangerous evil and the precious babies using their powers to deflect the evil cloud of destruction. The Son beast released His power, letting out a great roar that shook the sky, then the Father beast let out a greater roar that shook the island and the sky, and The Great Spirit beast joined the babies in the sky fighting the great storm with rays of spiritual light, and the great black clouds begin to move back over the open waters. Then the Great Spirit beast shot rays of light toward Willowiest that intercepted their satellites. And the dark clouds hovering over Promise moved out back over the sea and toward Willowiest Island. Once it was over Willowiest the clouds burst open rains of fires and sharp burning spears, which fell onto the island. The entire inhabitance of Willowiest was destroyed. The island of Promise was saved. Little Mercy, Grace, and Favor flew earthward quickly back to the safety of Marley, Perfect, and Patsy's arms. Perfect hugged her little tight. She said, I'm so proud of all of you to help safe our home the way you did. Marley smiled at the babies and said, they are good little warriors for righteousness already. The great beast stood on the mountainside looking down at its newest inhabitance of Promise. Then they spoke for the first time. The Father beast spoke first. And as He spoke the great beast of the fields bowed down their heads. Theirkinds we know why you are here and we welcome you. When you came onto this

island, your lives have been transformed. You are new creatures. And you only qualification is love and belief. And you
all passed the test. You are home now if you wish to live here.
Trouble can no longer follow you only you can choose to follow trouble. No one will harm you are here. This is a place of
divine peace, love, and fellowship. I am the Father this is my
Son and this is the Great and only Holy Spirit. If you choose
to stay here, we request one thing and that is to believe in us
the power of the Father, the Son, and the Holy Spirit. And
we will always protect all of you. We will teach you our ways if
you so desire to learn them. Come as you are and we will give
you peace and rest. We offer eternal life here. As you are welcomed to stay you are welcomed to leave. Here no one is held
against their will. If you choose to stay with us. You will be
making a wise choice. Because you will be loved completely
and equally. We know where you came from, in order to run
from something means that you are running to something.
This island you call Promise is blessed. And all the inhabit-
ances are blessed. Thank you for bringing our children
home. Always know that Mercy, Grace, and Favor brought
you here and they will always be with you. And they can never
lead you where the Father, the Son, and the Holy Spirit can't
protect you. Go in peace about your lives and enjoy your new
home. Be blessed and have faith. And they disappeared into
the mountain top. Just then, a small boat appeared over the
horizon, in the distance on the water. Who else but Sin had
returned she slowly approached the shore of Promise. The
great beast of the fields, kept watch by the shores. They sensed
the evil that approached them. As her boat touched the shore

line. The sand started to burn the side of the boat. The great beast of the field started growling and would not allow her enter. One beast spoke and said go away from us. For you filled with defiled spirits and evilness. Be gone! Go away for you are not welcomed on this island. Sin turned her yacht around and went back out over the water. She docked out about 150 yards out with a bull horn yelling. HEY AH I NEED SOME HELP HERE. HEY GUYS WILLOWIEST IS DESTROYED AH I DON'T HAVE ANY PLACE ELSE TO GO! HEY PERFECT, CLUEY, NERVIUS. HEY TELL'EM YOU ALL KNOW ME RIGHT. WE'RE ALL FRIENDS RIGHT! Talk to them. She waits a moment then she gets mad. You all know you need me there. I'M SIN YOU CAN'T LEAVE ME OUT. EVERYBODY NEEDS ME. HEY WHAT IS ANY PLACE WITHOUT ME? LIFE IS BORING WITHOUT ME! YOU NEED ME. She paces back and forth on her boat. WHAT ARE YOU'RE GOING TO DO ABOUT FEAR? THAT'S WHAT MAKES LIFE FUN. HEY I'M TRYING TO SHOW YOU PEOPLE HOW TO LIVE HERE!! HEY WHAT ABOUT HATRED! WE CAN'T LET EVERYBODY IN. WHAT ABOUT JEALOUSY! WHAT ABOUT DOUBT! WHAT ABOUT LUST! NO ONE CAN LIVE WITHOU THAT. . WHAT ABOUT DECIET! YOU ALL KNOW YOU NEED ME! YOU KNOW IT. YOU KNOW WHAT YOU ALL ARE JUST A BUNCH OF BORING DUMB ASSES. YOU DON'T NEED ME AND I DON'T NEED YOU. She quiets down for a few moments. Come on guys who wants to really live in a world without ME. WHAT ABOUT MONEY!

MONEY IS POWER! After she gets no response from the island she sits there with her arms folded pouting, talking to herself. Well I'll just have to make them like me. I will get on that island somehow. They'll see. I will get on that island. She cranks up her boat and sails away. AH HEY GUYS I HAVE TO GO NOW I'LL BE BACK.

I'll BE BACK!

Back cover

"Their- kinds"

"Exciting, spiritual, and mystical"

This has more turns than a tennis match.

There are three species on Willowiest Island and they better know their place

The Elites One eyed Theirkinds

━ ～

The Middle class Two eyes $

━ ～

The Lower class Three eyes s

"THERE WILL BE NO INTERACTING WITH ONE ANOTHER, NO DATING, NO FRIENDSHIPS, NO MARRYING. NO MATING STAY AMONG YOUR ON KIND FOR IT IS THE LAW"

THE ELITEST THEIRKINDS the One eye's only concern is to apply the law through greed, power, and control. Their laws are in place to benefit the few and control the many. Social segregation between them are strong. And no one dares cross that line. But that line was crossed.

About the Author

Retha Richardson is a native of Atlanta, Georgia. Inspired to write by her faith, Richardson has used storytelling to pursue new ideas and goals she had never before thought possible.

Richardson firmly believes that it's never too late to chase your dreams.